GUYS LIKE ME

Dominique Fabre

Translated by
Howard Curtis

NEW VESSEL PRESS
NEW YORK

GUYS LIKE ME

▮New Vessel Press

www.newvesselpress.com

First published in French in 2007 as *Les types comme moi*
Copyright © 2007 Librairie Arthème Fayard
Translation Copyright © 2015 New Vessel Press

This work, published as part of a program providing publication
assistance, received financial support from the French Ministry of
Foreign Affairs, the Cultural Services of the French Embassy in the
United States and FACE (French American Cultural Exchange).

French Voices Logo designed by Serge Bloch.

Library of Congress Cataloging-in-Publication Data
Fabre, Dominique
[*Les types comme moi* English]
Guys Like Me/ Dominique Fabre; translation by Howard Curtis.
p. cm.
ISBN 978-1-939931-15-3
Library of Congress Control Number 2014946429
I. France -- Fiction

1

HIS EYES WERE BLUE, FROM WHERE I WAS. HE LOOKED
tired. He looked as if he'd been waiting there for a long
time, although that was impossible. Neither of us could
have known in advance which way we'd be going that day.
I'm a mature man, I'm fifty-four, but in some respects I'll
never be mature enough. For example, the way I sometimes get scared when I meet someone. Mostly you just
run into people, and it doesn't lead to anything. Actually, our lives are full of things that lead to other things,
and it's hard to believe that in this case it hadn't led to
anything in all those years. But he looked familiar, from
where I was. From where I was, it might still have been
possible, somehow, to turn around and walk away, even
though obviously I would never have turned around and
walked away of my own accord. But a car might have
started, in which case I'd have had to get out of the way,
or I might have looked the other way and not seen his
reflection in a shop window. I'd have reacted by saying to
myself what does that guy want with me? And I'd probably have ignored him, I'd probably have forgotten him.
His face looked drawn, but his hair wasn't gray. I've almost lost my hair. Sometimes I run my hand through it,
and there's nothing there. My ex-wife used to laugh when
I did that, and I don't think I took it well. I don't like
taking a wrong turn, but it'd be right to say that when we
met again we'd both taken a wrong turn. Maybe our lives,

too: lots of wrong turns placed end to end, you can never reconstruct the whole journey.

...

His clothes were almost as all-purpose as mine. He'd been wearing them longer than I had. His shoes were polished, in spite of the wear and tear. At that moment, he'd already resumed his place in my life, and I in his. But had we ever really been friends? He was carrying a computer case, and of course I could never have imagined how important it was in his life. It was a long time since he'd last had his own things, in his life, and he kept all those papers in his case, in an ashamed kind of way. He was pretending too. He'd always pretended, I told myself later, remembering things from long ago. But I wasn't so sure of that in the days that followed. His eyes were blue, and he was carrying that fake case. By the time we were pushing thirty, his good times were already behind him, as far as I knew. He'd already had a beautiful wife, a beautiful apartment, and we'd stopped seeing each other except from time to time, although I often felt like calling him. I didn't know why he was where he was. He didn't tell me, he was long past explaining things. Try to find out what happened, and you never get the answers you want. Try to figure out how the earth turns, how people live and die, notice the changes on the streets, and there's too much missing, when you get down to it. How are you doing? Neither of us said things like that, things like, how many years has it been? What have you been doing with yourself all this time? He didn't have time for things like that, with his case in his hand. All he said was hey, I thought it was you.

"Me too. It is Jean, isn't it?"

"Yes, don't you recognize me?"

"Yes, yes, of course I do."

We shook hands, didn't say any more, just carried on walking together. We were in the area near the station, where I almost never go, not since I moved. But for no particular reason, I sometimes make a detour and go back there, stay an hour, without talking to anyone.

• • •

He didn't live in the neighborhood anymore either. There was a time when he hadn't lived anywhere in particular, to be honest. A day here, three nights there, even sometimes in hotels that didn't have names, only street numbers, surrounded by recent Eastern European immigrants and the customary Arab, he was a bit old for that. We walked back up the street, without meaning to we found ourselves going in the same direction, the two of us. We sat down in a café on Rue d'Amsterdam, pretty much halfway along the street. A place where for a long time now, maybe forever, people have been crossing diagonally to gain a few seconds, on this side of the street, on the way toward one of the side entrances to the train station, near the big post office. It was because of his case that I realized. How could a guy like that get to this point? I'm not the only one to ask myself that question, not that he talked much about it. His hands also seemed as if they came from another time. It's crazy, but that's how it is. We were at the back of the café, where it was dimly lit. Above the bar were posters advertising special offers, the week's happy-hour cocktails. That kind of thing shows me I'm from another time really. I'll never be able to manage. Every time that idea comes into my head, I get scared, I don't know what to do to get rid of that feeling. Although sometimes, I like it. They didn't have happy hours in the bars we used to go to together in the old days. There was a time when I often went to England for my work, and there too, I noticed it, time must have passed everywhere, often in the same way. In the light of the booth, his face looked drawn. He was carrying a shadow with him, along with all the rest, the lines, the deep marks left by our lives. Which of us was the first to ask what the other wanted to drink? I can't remember. I'd really like to remember everything, I might be able to trace the crack he'd slipped through, the crack through which he left again, even if I couldn't help him. I like helping people, though, in life. I'm not a good Samaritan, or a bad one, it's the way I was born, period. How can I explain it?

He didn't talk at first. He looked as if he needed rest. He also seemed to be contemplating something, a kind of map of his life, a whole bunch of forks in the road, our encounter being one path, or a kind of crossroads. I don't know how to talk about these things. We don't like to say these things. But we see them in the faces of the people we meet. The fact is, nothing about these things changes with time. For years, they've been giving tents to poor people so that they don't die of cold during the night. But we weren't in winter anymore, so why did I think of that when I saw him? He was clasping his case to his chest, sitting on the imitation leather banquette. He'd insisted on my taking the banquette, as if that was still one of the generous gifts he could afford. But I played a stupid game with him, without even being aware of it, and said I had to go take a leak. He nodded slowly, with a big, cracked smile, and finally took his place on the banquette. When I came back upstairs, I saw him sitting there with his case clasped tightly to his chest. A steel cannabis leaf in the colors of the Jamaican flag was hanging from the zipper, and later I saw a whole bunch of guys like him and me with cannabis leaves in the colors of the Jamaican flag, but not all of them were down on their luck. I sometimes feel like telling jokes, like with him. He was waiting for me to say something, as if he really wanted me to take responsibility for the stupidity of this reunion.

"Let me look at you."

I said that, or maybe I didn't, but from that first time, I could never look at him enough, a bit like when you're in love, and you'd like to have a woman's face and body permanently in front of your eyes, so as not to offend them. Of course I thought he'd changed a lot. Maybe we both simultaneously recalled dates and events, memories we could have shared. He didn't open up in that café, didn't relax his smile. But I recognized him when he jutted out his lower lip and blew upwards. That was something he always used to do when we were teenagers. Maybe that stupid gesture was something he thought was seductive, the way other people use their smiles.

"Do you ever hear from André?"

He stopped smiling. André was another guy with blue eyes and a smile. André Lebars? Yes, that's the one. He made a face, no, he hadn't heard from him lately. Why should he care about him anyway? That was kind of the impression he gave me at that moment. He didn't want anyone standing between us, I sensed then that he'd decided to hit me up for a loan.

It started when I turned forty, like most guys I know. I sponsor a little orphan, a little Haitian boy as it happens, and every year I keep the letter he sends me, a completely stereotypical letter to the white man who sends him a check for twenty-five euros every month. A year after my divorce, I also started volunteering in a hospital, but that way of doing good didn't suit me all that much, because often, the next day, I'd start to feel symptoms, and more than once I fell ill. How can you give a hand to someone who's dying anyway? I never figured out the answer to that. There were support groups too, with shrinks, only it bored me, and I stopped, it wasn't my thing. Then I met a woman I was hoping to get love from, but nothing like that happened. I was forty-four when I discovered that you can hope to get love in return for a washing machine, two installments on a car, and other things like that. When I realized that, I was cured of that woman, and of others too in the long run. I wasn't seeing much of Benjamin at the time. Just after our separation, I tried to live close to him, I'd call him every two or three days, but even during the times when he needed me I often disturbed him. So I found myself calling him less often, he was growing up. I'm very proud of him, he's done well so far. But I can't say anything about that pride because I think all I've done is pay, since he was eleven, and he's twenty-six now. I missed all that, I sometimes tell myself. He soon got into the habit of living with a sporadic father, his mother didn't set him against me too much, I let things go during the divorce proceedings in order not to hurt them. Two years later was the time of the woman with the installments who needed a washing machine, a time also of unemployment and depression, and I couldn't pay the alimony in time. A bailiff came at seven in the morning. I've never dared to ask Benjamin if his mother told him.

• • •

He looked around him from time to time. The waiters were young, there was a blonde woman in black behind the cash register, looking at her cell phone. She couldn't have been much more than thirty. She kept up an amused conversation with each of the guys coming and going between the bar and the back room. We were in one of the booths, the kind that seemed meant especially for people on their own. He often walked past this café, he told me later. I can't really remember when he told me that. It was still one of the pleasures he could afford on Rue d'Amsterdam. It wasn't the only one, obviously. But apart from the papers in the case for his laptop, which he'd also had to sell, he had almost nothing left. He'd found a little ground-floor apartment, which he rented in La Garenne-Colombes. I offered him a cigarette to replace the words we didn't say during that first meeting. He took it without thinking, with two white fingers that must have made me think of the claws of a bird of prey. I often lack imagination, so when I talk about myself I can't help talking about him, and when I talk about him I'm talking about me. Because it was him, because it was me. I learned that in class, was I still sitting at the same desk as him, or next to Marc-André? Anyway, it stayed with me. It's the same with Martin Luther King's speech, *I Have a Dream*, and also *Tired of Waiting*, we must have been in eighth grade. He'd left school. His mother had found a job in Marseilles, they'd lived there for a year. Then when he came back, we talked again, but we didn't have the same life anymore, and he wasn't at school. He lit it greedily, as if he'd been craving it for a long time. Cigarettes are expensive.

"Do you still smoke?"

I smiled, without meaning to.

Yes, even though I'm over fifty I still smoke, though less than before.

"Five a day, something like that," I said, as if I needed to justify myself to him.

He didn't seem to be listening. But even though he didn't look as if he was listening, I had plenty of time to realize that he hadn't forgotten any of the things I'd said to him, or done for him. We smoked for a while in silence. A couple came and sat down in the booth next to ours, in the tinted light, which seemed to come from a fluorescent tube. The waiter took our orders. I was thinking about Benjamin, what was he up to right now? Sometimes, in all those years, I thought I was going to see him, turning a corner in Paris, without our having talked. And so, because I wanted it so much to happen, when he did see me it came at the right time, he'd been feeling sad, or he'd even been thinking about me. Not about his monthly check, or his cell phone contract, like when he was starting out in life, but about me, his father. He looked at the end of his cigarette and asked me if I'd ever been to Cuba. No, I'd never been to Cuba. Still haven't.

"You never liked traveling."

He was the same as he'd always been, ever since he was a child, obsessed with traveling. I pushed him further on this. "How about you, still roaming?"

He shook his head. He looked toward the couple we'd seen come in when we'd sat down. "A bit, but after a while, you know ..."

He made a broad gesture that ended in mid-air, just like that.

"Did you get tired of it?"

I wanted to set my mind at rest about his love of traveling, which had been with him since childhood.

"After a while, you know ... You can't spend your whole life traveling, you need to set down roots somewhere."

I nodded, I think. I have roots, I told myself later. But what could that mean to a guy like him?

"I'd like to be able to go back to Africa one last time."

I immediately remembered the book in his bedroom when we were children.

"By the way, how's your mother?"

He didn't seem surprised by my asking him about his mother. In fact, he even seemed pleased.

"Not bad for her age."

He leaned slightly in the direction of the bar. Outside, the noise of the crowd walking down toward Cour du Havre. The same noise for years. I've often forgotten it.

"I don't see much of her, she lives in an apartment in

Marseilles, with a cousin of hers. But she's fine, I mean, she forgets a lot of things."

"In Marseilles?"

"Yes, the rents are too high in Paris. She has a cousin down there, they share a small apartment. They're old now. Do you know what I mean?"

I said yes, of course I know what you mean.

I already knew that later, when I got home, other fragments of the story we shared would come back to me from time to time and keep me awake. I'd always liked his mother even though, like mine with me, we both knew they didn't need us in their lives, and that in some way we were like enemies because we'd been born. His mother was the concierge of an apartment building, and also worked as a cleaner. In the evening, sometimes, she'd go dancing with her friends in clubs in Argenteuil, La Garenne, and Paris. She loved dancing. He'd go with her, as soon as he became a teenager. I remembered I envied him that. Now the couple was embracing, what age could they be? When the guy listened to her talking, that little blonde with extensions, he'd look up at the ceiling, with a smile on his lips, his body strained toward her. My wife took the decision to get a divorce after reading an American book called *Mars Versus Venus*. Or something like that. She only ever read in bed, slowly. For three months, that book was on the coffee table in the living room. Benjamin also noticed it. I don't know why the scenes of happiness that I see, in cafés or elsewhere, always remind me of that book lying on the coffee table in the living room all that time, and I'm not able to wipe out the memory.

"Did you see Mom's book?"

"Yes, Benjamin, it'd have been hard not to see it."

I must have given him some kind of awkward answer like that, it was already thirteen years ago.

"Why don't you talk to her? Don't you know what to

say to her? Why?"

I remember I took it badly at the time. He was angry, he already knew what was going to happen. I asked him to shut up, and later, when the two of us were alone, my son and I, I tried to explain. But I couldn't find the words, and as for him, he was busy tapping away on his computer, he didn't want to talk about it anymore.

"You're right, it's none of my business."

And so I didn't tell him.

• • •

When we finally stopped looking at each other and looking away, when he took another cigarette from the pack and, as if we were regulars there, I made a sign to the waiter to bring us another drink, yes, that's right, the same, he started to tell me. Yes, he'd lost his job. I should have suspected it; he didn't make a big thing about it, except that he was over fifty. I didn't ask him any questions, the whole time he was talking to me. Yes, the whole time he was talking to me that day, I don't think I came up with more than two sentences, because I'd immediately sensed how much he needed it. He really had given a lot of himself to the job. He'd followed all the technical changes, and he spoke German reasonably well. That wasn't an obvious thing for a guy like him who hadn't had much schooling. He quite simply hadn't seen it coming. Of course, you just had to switch on the TV to know, but he didn't think it would happen to him, not to him. The worst thing was, he hadn't put any money aside. He'd helped his mother with the apartment in Marseilles with her cousin, and now he was renting a really small ground-floor apartment. A man had a lot of debts in life, that's what life meant. He came out with two or three things like that, without knowing it. Without knowing it, he was painting a picture of a guy who could have been me, or so many others, but who was actually him. He didn't get worked up as he told me. He occupied his days as best he could, he'd asked all his acquaintances to keep their eyes and ears open, because at his age they were the only people he could count on. He called it being humanly alert. I remember that awkward expression, where had he dug it up? His last partner had left him, he'd become unbearable, she kept telling him, unbearable, that was the excuse she'd given, but in fact she didn't really care either way. She'd been with him out of a kind of self-interest, which she'd calculated pretty well, and seeing him unemployed had made up her mind for her.

"How old was she?"

"What? Oh, forty-seven, I think."

He seemed surprised by my question, as if it was of no interest. Then, just in his eyes, at that moment, I saw a boyish smile. Maybe he still loved her, or had never stopped? But no, not really. He'd gone to the employment court, not expecting anything from it. The guys who'd fired him were from the same generation as him, they were your age, he said. They knew perfectly well they were screwing him over, but getting rid of a few people like him might be worth it, they must have told themselves something like that. He'd been naive, and he'd been stupid, now he looked back on it, he really hadn't seen it coming.

He kept looking around us, around me, in the café. The booths had all filled up little by little, and there were more and more people out in the street, on their way to catch a train at the Gare Saint-Lazare. His case was full of papers, letters of confirmation, bailiff's notices, résumés to be sent or ones already returned, current business. He had an envelope with those words on it. He put it down on the table. He didn't open it, as if he was still hesitating. I had the premonition, that evening, thinking about it, that something else would happen in his life, that it wouldn't end there. Was it because of the computer case, emptied of its contents, where he kept his papers? Or was it the owner of the café, that young woman with the clear complexion who didn't give any impression of youth or life? Guys like me often feel really sad when they look at other people. Since I turned forty, and especially since my divorce, four years after that, my only consolation has been my work, which allows me to keep such things at a distance. Since my separation, I haven't had a real love affair. I don't have the strength for it anymore, I kept telling myself. But why would I need strength? How the time passes ... Quite often, my thinking stops there, and I try to sleep immediately afterwards, because I really don't know what's waiting for me if I keep thinking.

We saw each other a few times after that. What surprised me from the beginning was that thanks to him, because he also wanted to know about me, to know things about my life, to do part of the work and not be outdone, I started to understand my own life better, or rather to see the truth in the way I tell it to myself, on those bad nights when I know I won't be able to sleep and my apartment seems tiny and I feel as if I'm going to end up suffocating in it. He'd been unemployed for more than two years, I didn't ask him for details. When we left the bar on Rue d'Amsterdam, he handed me the résumés I asked for. I glanced at them, there was his place of birth, near La Garenne-Colombes, that was our suburb before, his and mine, and lots of other guys too. His résumé, as far as I could tell, seemed plausible enough, except that he'd probably never be able to find anything again, because of his age. He never changed his mind about that. I even ended up asking him over the phone: what was the point of carrying on trying if, deep down, he was convinced that he'd never get out of this mess, that it was too late for him?

"I'll pass them around, and we'll see what happens."

"Thank you."

He was looking at me and nodding, like a child waiting for it to pass, as if that thank you wasn't addressed to me. How many guys like me had he approached, old acquaintances, guys he hadn't seen in years? Then he closed his case and folded his hands over it, and I didn't know if that meant he wanted to go, or on the contrary to stay, his hands placed on the top of his case, forever incapable of choosing between the outside and here, where he could stay. You never knew with him.

"By the way, how are things in La Garenne-Colombes?"

A wicked smile gradually lit up his face. "Oh, La Garenne-Colombes. There aren't many guys left who are still interested in La Garenne-Colombes."

"Why do you say that?"

He smiled a bit more, I liked seeing him like that, he reminded me of that little boy in La Garenne-Colombes, near Place de Belgique, he never found his way back to school, but that was beside the point now.

"I went back there last year, well, maybe five or six months ago. I hardly recognized a thing, you know."

"Why don't you go see for yourself? You aren't far, are you?"

I didn't reply.

He watched me put his résumé away in my briefcase, the briefcase of a man who was still whole. We both knew, maybe at the same time, how pointless it was, given his age. But then, when I read it again that evening, I wasn't so sure.

"Will one be enough?"

We were both still standing there.

"I'll make copies."

He nodded. He showed me a flash drive he'd taken out of his pocket. It was red. That surprised me, coming from him, but after all why not? We were the generation of floppy disks in offices, and also of *Atomkraft? Nein, danke!* I suddenly remembered those little metal badges we carried on our school satchels and wore on the lapels of our jackets, bought from the flea market in Clignancourt or in fake American surplus stores. We all had them in high school. We'd walk along the streets of Asnières in our combat jackets covered with badges. He collected them, sometimes resold them, sometimes swapped them.

"Well," he said, "it was great to see you again, even if the circumstances could be better."

I couldn't help smiling. "Shall we have a bite to eat one of these days?"

He said yes, shall I call you or will you call me?

I didn't need to think too much, I said no, I'll call you, no problem, we can meet next week.

We shook hands before we left the bar. The young woman at the cash register said goodbye, her voice sounded dull and worn. Her hard features under her blonde hair, in a bar on Rue d'Amsterdam. He wasn't sad or depressed, that time, any more than the following times. Most of the time, he kept in good spirits. He was born like that, in good spirits. What was he doing that evening? He shrugged, one hand holding the empty case and the other in the pocket of his raincoat, as if he could have stayed like that for years.

"I'm going for a walk, I may catch a movie, now that I have the card."

He still had his boyish smile, he meant his unemployment card, stamped so that he could get discounts.

"So long, I'll call you."

Then I walked down the street without turning around. Anyone seeing us together might have thought that two old friends had just had a drink, and that these moments stolen from everyday life (work, a wife, the children already flown the nest) had been a sliver of pleasure in their lives. I mean guys who've known each other for more than thirty years, yes, that's it, much more than thirty years in fact. All things considered, I'd enjoyed seeing him again. Apart from that, I wasn't sure what else to think.

That evening, thanks to him, I went back home with an idea in my head, something important to do, I had to try to help him get work. If it was only up to me … That's the kind of crap I've often told myself, since I've been alone and no woman has spent the night with me. I went through his résumé, trying to cross-check. If I could believe what I was reading, things had started to go wrong for him in 1997, which was already quite a while ago. What was going on in my life that year? I can remember people, events, sometimes I can remember very clearly conversations Benjamin and I had twenty years ago, I can even quote what he said word for word. But I get confused about dates. 1997, I really can't remember what that year had been like for me. Jean had even worked abroad for a short time, in Germany, he knew the language, I remembered that. I thought about two or three people I could call, though I didn't hold out much hope. For a few years now, all the guys like me have been putting together résumés and distributing them conscientiously, knowing there isn't really any point. He runs into you suddenly, one way or another, the one who gives and the one who asks, and you never really know why you're on one side or the other. Why had he run into me near Cour du Havre on the occasion of an interview I'd twice postponed, rather than someone else who might not have recognized him? I thought of Marc-André, he might be interested, thinking about Germany. Then I put away his papers, I tried only not to think about him, in other words about me too, and also a few others, guys from my teenage years. The Hauts-de-Seine had changed a hell of a lot, but we were still alive, some of us still kept in touch, they didn't want to let it all go. In a very short time, you end up forgetting. Sometimes I remembered passionate conversations we'd had, he was there too, we'd been to the movies, they still sometimes had debates after the movie in those days. Was it Marc-André who'd worked for a sound engineer while he was studying? All of us knew already, even at the age of twenty, that the world we came from was in the process of disappearing, but we didn't think about it most of the time. I put his résumé away in my desk, where I spend a lot of time. Sometimes I bring back work, but most of the time I sit there and do nothing at all, it's next to the window.

...

At the start, Benjamin's mother and I lived in a two-room apartment, my office was in the bedroom, then, when he was ten, we moved, and I had a room specially for my office, but I didn't really use it. I've forgotten why, anyway. Nowadays, almost every day, I sit down at my desk for a while. When I get home from work, I sit down at my desk for five minutes, trying to relax, or else, in the morning, I often sit there briefly, for no reason. Something's waiting for me there, but what? As a result, my desk always seems like somebody else is inhabiting it, somebody else who's exactly like me. Saturday morning is when I read the newspaper. Sometimes, when I feel like it, I write letters. I have a photo of my son and me, he's thirteen, we're both in Collioure, I'm in the midst of separating from his mother, I'm trying not to let anything show. The weather is fantastic. I've put my laptop in the living room, I don't use it much. All I did was join a dating site, which I look at when I feel like it. A lot of people do that where I work, not all of them are married. The photograph on my profile is already a bit old, I can't make up my mind to change it. But in spite of that deception, all I've had are some pretty dull dates, women obsessed with their age, in a hurry to rebuild their lives. That's why I soon stopped putting on a show for most of my dates. I also have photos in the dresser, mainly of Benjamin. For a long time I tried not to look at them during the week, between the weekends, when I was allowed to see him, because they sometimes made me feel really bad. Anaïs asked me to show them to her. All three of us were moved. It was like looking at a life. I keep two of him in my wallet, one when he's about ten, we were both with his mother, and another taken at the Buttes-Chaumont park last year, he's with Anaïs and some other guys from the same biology lab, they're all lying on the grass. I filched it from him one evening when he and Anaïs invited me for dinner. Filched it like a little boy. I stayed there five minutes. Things were going poorly for him too. The country really wasn't working, you heard people say that more and more often, and I ended up believing it. Sometimes also, when I'm sitting at my desk, memories come to me, there are often good moments waiting for me. Or at other times, I expect the opposite, and I don't open the door to that room all weekend, in order not to spoil anything.

I'd enjoyed seeing him again. I hadn't asked him any questions, and in the end he hadn't told me much about himself. Maybe there was nothing to say. Things were the way they were. We'd only decided to have a drink together the following week. I hadn't suggested lunch, because I didn't have my appointments book with me. It was in my desk, I also have two personal organizers, and lots of others from past years. My mother used to keep them too. Sometimes, she'd cross out every page and write the important appointments in shorthand so that nobody would know what they were. Who could have known them? I knew all the initials in her life, and I could imagine who without wanting to. Much later, I started collecting movie tickets, I used to go quite often at one point, just after my divorce. I'd go directly from my office to the movie theater, when I wasn't invited over to friends', and immediately afterwards, when I got back, I'd take a shower and go straight to bed, with sleeping pills. That way I didn't have too much time to think about anything else. Of course, sometimes it didn't work, but anyway. I also collected business cards of all the guys I met, and one summer, I'd only been away for ten days with Benjamin, I placed them all in a row and glued them like that, it took me two days. I bought some glass mounts in Paris, and then spent two days on it. Why was I in that state? For a long time I looked at those cards without daring to hang them on the wall, and then, one day, a woman came to my apartment and looked at them in a strange way, and that was when I understood. Or rather, I didn't really understand, but since I wanted her to stick around, I realized that I probably had to do something else as far as decoration went. Sylvie. 1997. That was the year his résumé seemed to have the most gaps, not very well concealed. Eight years of hard times? 1997: Sylvie and I lived together for almost two years. We both made an effort, but in different directions, and in the end we drifted apart. And then she met a man who was a few years younger than her and fell "madly in love." I like that expression, I wrote it on a card I sent her from Martinique, with a question mark. That was dumb of me, obviously. She never replied to my question. Had I ever loved as much as she had? Had I ever been loved?

I can spend a whole weekend thinking like that. The first time I saw Jean was during a period when nothing was happening in my life. On Sunday evenings, Benjamin calls me. As soon as he calls, I offer to call him back. These days he says no, it's all right. We chat for a while. Sometimes I can feel his attention wandering, he doesn't really want to talk, often it's because he's had an argument with Anaïs and he's sulking, like I used to do with his mother, or else he's working on a project, and it's a real headache, as he puts it. When he was a kid, he loved poetry and drawing and I worried, without making a fuss about it, that he'd never really understand the kind of world he'd have to live his life in. I was wrong. Sometimes I feel sorry because of him, but most of the time, I'm proud. Too proud. I like his expressions, they come from his childhood, everything was always too something or other with him. Too good, too boring. He also tells me how his mother is, whether I like it or not. For a long time he clung to the idea that he'd see us together again, he's my only child. I guess I was once madly in love too.

On Saturday, I contacted my friend Marc-André, I called about eleven. He answered, he cleared his throat, the way he always does when he's going to speak.

"Hi, Marco, how's it going, hope I'm not disturbing you?"

This time, we didn't bother with small talk, just the minimum, he doesn't like the phone too much. I immediately told him the news, how I'd met Jean by chance on Rue d'Amsterdam, drifting, with his almost empty case. He was silent for a bit.

"Jean? Doesn't he have a job anymore?"

Then we talked about other things. He has four children, two of them with his second wife, Aïcha. They live in Levallois, like me, they bought a big apartment near the shopping mall, the living room is decorated in oriental style, that's where they receive their friends. It's like going on a journey but not very far, several thousand miles on a Friday evening, to Porte d'Asnières. His eldest daughter is studying medicine in Montpellier, but his son, his second child with his first wife, dropped out of college. Marco tells me about him from time to time. How he feels responsible, and yet he doesn't want to continue giving him checks to pay for his drugs. Once, because I've known him since he was born, I tried talking to Antoine. But I wasn't able to really tackle the subject. He reminds me of his father at the same age, he has the same somber, feverish look, that kind of energy and anger he gives off. He stopped without saying anything, as if he was used to it. I wasn't the first friend of his father he'd seen, and it hadn't helped at all. Where does he go when he seems to absent himself like that? Marc-André doesn't know. He's never known. He feels guilty because he thinks it happened when he met Aïcha.

He asked his son, his son replied no, don't worry about it. It was there before, it had always been there, and he didn't know why.

"I'm surprised," Marco said. "What a time we live in. He was in marketing, wasn't he?"

"Yes, he even worked in Germany."

"Does he speak the language?"

"Yes, he speaks German."

I heard him thinking on the other end.

"I don't know. I may be able to do something. Will you send me his résumé? Does he have an email address?"

I realized I'd forgotten to ask him. He was busy the next week, he was looking to see when he was free, I heard his wife behind him, the children were there too. Above that background noise, I could also sense that dark look of his, I'd say it's very human, though I'm not very sure why. Like when he talks about his first son or when he's been to visit him on his own, because Aïcha doesn't want to get involved, in the rehab clinic.

"It looks like it's going to be a crazy week," Marco said. "Can we speak again on Wednesday? I'll have a clearer idea then, maybe the three of us could get together?"

"Yes, if you like."

Then, very quickly, he hung up. I stayed in my office. I'm too old to change my job. Aren't there any new departures? There are no second acts. My son had that book, which I'd loved when I was a teenager. Yes, that was it. *There are no second acts.*

. . .

I sensed that today was going to be one more day of regrets. I don't like feeling like that, but I'd become incapable of fighting. It was building up inside me without my being able to do anything about it. I spent time in the bathroom. I cleaned the kitchen the way my mother used to forty years ago, and it was pointless because I'd already cleaned everything on Thursday evening and I hadn't invited anyone over this week. So I stopped and put away my broom and my stupid mop. I told myself I should keep trying, but what? They were the only words I knew, you must keep trying. Where had I learned that? Those dumb things? I couldn't make up my mind to go out.

The rain was coming in over the roofs from the Seine. We'd end up having almost no winter. I wasn't hungry. I'd had quite a lot of work that week, and I'd thrown myself into it without thinking about the weekend. I looked toward the end of my street, I have a three-room apartment. I finished paying it off one year ago. I should be happy, but I don't like Levallois much anymore, it's changed a hell of a lot in the last few years. I'm often one of those guys who can only say stuff like that, it seems, stuff like: it's completely changed, it's not the same at all, you can't recognize a thing. Of course, these thoughts are stupid, so I keep them to myself. I still sometimes dream about someone to share them with, a woman who'd understand what they mean.

They're an old man's thoughts, Benjamin says. I know he's right. I've never told him that they've been lurking inside me ever since I was a child. Who else could I have told them to? I went to see a shrink not long after my divorce. It was because I'd heard so many bad things said about me ... I'm joking, obviously. In fact, I just wanted to understand why, after I'd let things go for many years, after I'd accepted that life I was so ill-suited to, based on lies and convention. There are no second acts. But I still believe there are, from time to time. I wouldn't have the courage to go out this Saturday, the office had tired me out too much, I might do some shopping late in the afternoon. I'd pass guys like me, you also see us, younger ones, waiting at the ends of platforms, in large stations, at the beginning and end of the school vacations. What was the name of the guy I hit it off with, so to speak, the year Benjamin and his mother spent in the south, near Marseilles? She'd found a job with an open-ended contract and had decided to put as much distance as possible between her and me, and particularly between Benjamin and me, I think. That wasn't a good time for me.

I tried to distract myself, I might have a phone call or else what? I switched on the computer, checked the world news on the home page, then went on the dating website. I really should change my photo, I told myself. Years spent on that thing, it's not so easy to have a real date. You talk, you get excited, and the next day you're really not sure who it was. I looked at the new members. Some people subscribed to different sites, I wondered what the point of that was. You recognized their photos, even when they had different usernames. Of course, there was an enormous loneliness there, it was like a kind of ocean, the messages people sent each other hummed with it. These last few years, I'd met two or three women who were real culture vultures, and I'd run away after the sixth exhibition or the fifth museum. There had also been a woman I liked, ten years younger than me, but she'd taken off after three dates, and I couldn't blame her. She sent me a long recorded message two weeks later, the gist of which was that she was looking for somebody better than me, a younger guy who could be the father of her children. Three women I'd slept with, without hope or despair, just like that. I've often hurt myself thanks to the computer. I've probably hurt others too. But what else can you do? I chatted for an hour, thinking about Marc-André. He'd been braver than me, he'd been strong enough to start all over again from scratch. It hadn't been hard for him to decide when he met Aïcha. I closed the computer after an exhausting conversation about the musical tastes of a woman who told me how to download the pieces she liked. She had a really dumb username, Myosotis, she worked in the medical field. Goodbye, Myosotis. I wasn't likely to see her again with a handle like that. I still hadn't made up my mind to go out. I didn't get a phone call until six in the evening. I read for a while, and then, from my little balcony, I watched a few lights coming on down on the street three floors below. I saw people going out for a stroll because it had stopped raining and they were taking advantage, the time often passes for no reason.

Benjamin called me. I was pleased to hear from him. Twice in these last few years, we've had an argument and stopped seeing each other for six months: those were some of the hardest times in my life. He was doing OK. They were doing OK. Nothing new since the previous week. How about you, what have you been up to? I told him I was resting, oh, no, everything was fine. Nothing to worry about. We chatted some more. They were going to go on a long trip, he and Anaïs, they were thinking of the United States. How is Anaïs? Oh, she's fine. That was all he told me about her. One thing leading to another, we ended up talking about books, what was the name of that guy? That book where he says there are no second acts? Don't you remember? I sensed him thinking at the other end of the line, as if it was important to him not to disappoint me. F. Scott Fitzgerald. Oh, yes, that's it, F. Scott Fitzgerald, thanks. Why are you thinking about him? Benjamin asked. I don't know, I replied. It just came into my mind, no reason. Oh, right. He paused for a moment, then talked again about their plan, in two years' time they might drive along Route 66 with some friends of theirs, or else they'd rent a van, set off from San Antonio, take two weeks, go all the way up to the Great Lakes.

"How did you choose those particular places?"

He gave a low laugh. "I've just been looking at the map."

He wasn't alone with me anymore.

"All right, say hello to her for me, Ben. Speak again?"

"Sure, during the week."

"Bye, have a good Sunday."

I put down the phone and sat on the couch. There are no second acts, you know. Did he want to know why? You're smoking a cigarette, do you love me? Yes, I love you, I wonder why he asked me that. Hey, are you listening to me? Yes. Of course I am. I'm listening to you, kiss me. One Saturday evening. When I was able to stop thinking, I closed the door of my apartment, I left the lights on in order not to come back in the dark later. It's totally dumb, but I've never liked it to be dark when I get home.

...

I walked to the river bank. There were quite a lot of people about, and outside the florist's on the boulevard the cars were double-parked, people were stopping to buy bouquets of flowers before going to see their friends. I almost never take my car now. I have an old Renault 5, but don't dare take long rides in it. I like buying flowers from time to time. A guy was waiting in a Citroën CX, smoking a cigarette and turning the dial of his car radio. Was it that pretty brunette he was waiting for? I'd felt better since my son had called me. In ordinary weather, I'd have turned around once I got to the river bank, but now I carried on walking, there was nobody waiting for me at home. Sometimes, you're so alone you think you're talking aloud even when you haven't said a word. I walked for at least an hour and then stopped for a drink. I didn't stay long in the café. This Saturday was one of those days when I hadn't really lived, I'd just basically bided my time. Waiting for what? Tomorrow? Outside, there was laughter, loud voices, reflections. The line outside the convenience store that was probably used by people who lived in the apartment block opposite, a little way back from the road that ran along the river bank. I could probably have gone to the movies as a way to face Saturday evening, but I didn't really feel up to it, not even something as reliable as the movies. I generally chose particular theaters rather than particular movies. I liked to go to the places we used to go, I mean the places where we used to meet as friends, all those years ago. I'd go to the Pasquier Saint Lazare and the Ciné Caumartin, the one where they used to show porn movies up until the early '80s … I was living too much in my old memories on Saturday evening. There are no second acts. But over the past few years, what have I still had left of all that time? I tried not to think too much. When you're alone it's hard not to think about all that. I left quickly, as soon as I finished my beer. Sunday. Sunday and then Monday.

I had to run to pick up the phone.

"It's Jean. Am I disturbing you?"

"No, I just got in. Is everything OK? Wait, let me close

the door."

I grabbed the receiver again.

"What's going on? Is anything wrong?"

He didn't answer at first. "No, everything's fine. I just wanted to thank you."

His voice seemed to come from very close by, completely isolated from the world, if you can say that.

"Don't mention it. I was really pleased to see you."

"Me too."

Two strangers, sometimes, who compete at seeing who can be most attentive and polite, try to meet, and never say goodbye again. I should have stopped him once and for all. Of course, I knew: no second acts, I'd been thinking about that on the way back from the river bank, and I didn't like the idea. Yes, I was sure we could meet this week. Hadn't we already talked about that in the café? I had a few people in mind for his résumé. He seemed to be on the verge of telling me something. But in the end he was evasive, just as if he'd called me to reassure himself, to count me among those he could call for no reason. I didn't tell him about Marc-André. Just as abruptly as he'd called me, basically to say nothing, he said goodbye and I didn't even have time to reply. I switched on the computer. I went on the dating website, and then changed my mind, Myosotis, what a handle, really! I switched to Google and typed in F. Scott Fitzgerald. I'd loved his work when I was young, I think I'd read it in school. There are no second acts. He had a tendency to drink to excess, and he was jealous of Ernest Hemingway, they were two guys comparing their bank accounts, their successes with women, and their masculinity. He was bad at spelling and he never gave up. He believed in happiness, he never spared himself. He died at the age of forty-seven. I printed out his biography. I was going to re-read his books. I ate an apple standing up in the kitchen, I took a couple of pills, I wasn't tired enough yet. Most of the lights in the windows opposite were off by the time I went to bed. It was two in the morning.

I have nothing to say about the following day. The sky was gray, with a little sun. I went to see the Seine, which is often my friend on Sunday mornings. It was gray and didn't seem angry with me. I went for a walk around the old places, I saw the little park where Benjamin took his first steps. Square Max de Nansouty, it's called. There were young parents and children with snotty noses. Smiles and black, green, blue eyes. I saw the windows of our old two-room apartment, and to my surprise I didn't feel anything. Was that my first act, that period? At least I no longer resented my ex-wife. Now she was only the mother of my son, she'd stopped being the woman who'd done everything to deprive me of him and to screw me out of everything she could get from me. I'd forgotten precisely what it was that had made the two of us so unhappy. Back to the park. I used to go jogging along the river bank. A cardiologist had advised it. I'd stopped that fall, I was pissed off at always being overtaken by people who were faster than me.

At home, I looked for someone to call, I didn't want to disturb Benjamin, I took a shower and wondered what to do. I looked at the computer, it was gathering dust on the low table. I caught myself hoping that one day, one day, it would finally be time for me to put it away in my desk, it would merely be an accessory in my life. I knew so many guys like me, who had met women like them and deluded themselves it was real. I thought about him, about our childhood. Was it because I'd been walking in the old places? His mother and he had left for Marseilles, I think it was for one year, they'd both changed. She was a concierge. Then, after high school, he'd left for Hamburg, and I continued my studies at Paris University. One day, you can't go on, all you know is that time's passing, that life's too short, and that there are no second acts. In general it grabs hold of me very late at night, when I can't sleep and I don't have the courage to get up. I do my ironing if I have any. My shirts are often neat, my pants properly creased. When I'm older, in a few years, I'll have to find a few clubs to join, to keep myself occupied. I didn't want to spend Sundays alone any more. Then I thought about him. There were a few things on his résumé I found hard to understand. Any employer would probably feel the same.

I let the phone ring for a long time, he couldn't have been at home. I kept remembering without wanting to. While minding my own business, my mother used to say. Why did I remember that? I went out to buy bread, there was a line of people waiting to buy cakes for Sunday. I made myself some vegetable soup. I like it, and when I get back late from the office all I have to do is heat up a bowl of it. Finally, I called Myosotis, what a dumb handle she had. But she had a nice voice, I found, and she was funny too. What was I doing, playing cat and mouse? It's that username, I said, don't you have a real name?

"Marie, my name's Marie. Is that better for you?"

She had a kind of laugh behind her voice. We talked for a while. Had she had any dates? Yes, of course, but I surely wasn't calling her to ask her that? I hung up an hour later, I hadn't been aware of the time passing. I almost felt like calling her again and telling her that no guy like me could call Myosotis again, that was for sure. We'd see each other soon, of course, if you like. You know where to reach me. I found another book by F. Scott Fitzgerald. It wasn't the one with the second act, it was the story about the guy who's always asking if he can pull down the curtain. I told myself that one day I wouldn't be able to stand Sundays anymore.

2

THERE HE WAS, IN FRONT OF ME, IN MY OFFICE. I'D HAD A call from the switchboard to announce him, by that time I'd forgotten all about him. He was sitting in the hallway behind the picture window, a guy quietly waiting for his appointment. I suddenly thought of him as an intruder, though I couldn't quite get used to seeing him in that light. His case between his legs, a picture of defeat. But in my head that day there was sunshine, and I was in a good mood. I showed him in without waiting. Then I closed the door behind us.

"Hi. I was in the area. I wanted to see where it was, to get an idea."

"Come in, you did the right thing. Have you heard from Marc-André?"

I pointed to a seat. Often, in our lives without second acts, especially in the office, it seems to me that lots of guys like me imitate soap operas, but how to do otherwise? He put his black case down on his right, like earlier in the hallway. His eyes, still as blue and tired of looking.

"Yes, he sent me a note, and then he called to ask for my e-mail."

He was looking around him with a curious, almost cheerful gaze. That he didn't feel this place was completely devoid of warmth made me want to smile. Plus, I was pleased with myself.

"By the way, look, I have this for you to do if you're

interested."

The translator my firm usually called was on maternity leave. It was a legal contract, forty pages long, nobody had the time to do it here. It wasn't very complicated, at least I didn't think it was.

"Are you sure?"

"Yes, will it be OK? Is it up your alley? I have some documentation to help you. You can re-use a few things."

He opened the folder like a guy opening a book telling him the main events still to come in his life. He nodded as he looked through the pages, as if he'd already guessed them.

"I know these things, it isn't the first time I've seen contracts like this."

His fingers were long and white. He seemed pleased, but no more than that. Did I want to get rid of him now? You'd like to help, give them a chance, but really, when it comes down to it, you want them to go, as far from you as possible, and, in such cases, if they cross your path again, you barely have time to say hello, all bright and breezy, you promise to meet again soon, lunch, a drink, whatever.

Outside, there was only a little sunshine, I asked if it'd be all right. Yes, it'd be all right. When was it for? He told me he was sorry he'd just showed up like that, no, no, I was going to call you about this anyway. The office returned to the forefront as soon as I passed him the technical documentation for the previous contracts. He wouldn't actually have many new things to translate. So, when was it needed by? He stood up. We talked mainly about Marc-André and Aïcha, he knew her, he thought, from an office where she'd temped while finishing her psychology studies. It's a small world. Those were my glory days, he murmured. He made me smile, with his dumb expression. He put the file and the documentation away in his case. He'd emptied it since the last time in the café. He probably made it ready every day. He closed it as if an important secret was hidden in it, one that he was taking home with him. He held out his hand.

"Thank you. It was a good thing I dropped by."

"Yes. That's true."

I don't know why I had the impression at the time that I'd done something really stupid, for no reason. I walked downstairs with him, and watched him leave, he was in a hurry, his head bent as if there was too much wind. I smoked a cigarette. The week passed quickly.

I saw Benjamin on Tuesday evening, coming out of work. We had dinner together in a crêperie in Montparnasse, Anaïs was currently temping in the area. She finished at ten o'clock. These days, the hours I spend with my son, even the best ones, are limited. Actually, they have been since our separation. She herself was always late, which was why we often had arguments, but from the start she'd wait for Benjamin to come back with her eye on the clock. I'd receive registered letters about that, right from the start of the separation. One day, I wanted to tell my son, you know what I'd really like? I'd like us to spend a week together, with Anaïs if she's OK with it, and we could go anywhere we liked, we wouldn't have a set time and we wouldn't be waiting for anything in particular. We wouldn't be stressed by you having to pack your bag, like when you were a child and you had to go and we'd realize at the last minute you'd forgotten things. Do you remember? Anaïs came out of the offices in the tower, we chatted for five minutes. It was too late to go to the movies, and besides she was hungry. We'll talk on the phone. Yes, *ciao*.

I'd stopped thinking about Jean. Marc-André had called him to clarify a few points. He had a new e-mail address, he went to check his mail in an internet café in Colombes, not far from the station. By the way, was I free on Friday? Yes, I was free. Of course I was free. He told me he might have some good news for him, but it wasn't really certain. Should we invite him on Friday too, then the three of us would be together? Yes, why not? Friday arrived without mishap. He'd called me at the office, but I had an outside meeting, I think, visiting clients. Marie didn't go online every evening, I wondered if she was sulking, but because of what? I even wandered onto the other sites, where could you find love after the age of fifty? Nothing in the newspaper. Nothing on the cork noticeboard at work either, nothing anywhere. I burned the songs she'd sent me and listened to them in my room in the evening. Cesaria Evora. They were really beautiful. A woman who lived near Place Clichy was haunting my dreams. Well, why not? I read F. Scott Fitzgerald, around ten at night, when I wasn't too tired. A few pages. Do you mind if I pull down the curtain? I didn't worry all that much, behind my open shutters, they were never closed. I was feeling quite good that week. I thought about Marie, which just goes to show. The weather was gradually improving. I even slept all night and woke up with an erection in the morning. What woman could I have been dreaming about? When I was a teenager, I thought I'd be able to talk about these things, but when it came down to it, they were always going to be there, floating in front of me, and I'd never be able to grab hold of them, never be able to escape them. A whole lifetime.

I made some phone calls on Friday afternoon. I'm well known in the business, but most of the guys I contacted were surprised I was calling them, especially on a Friday. Yes, they were already in the loop. Marco had called them. Or he'd called them himself, and with some of them their voices turned a bit too grim when they told me that, and what about you, how are you?

"I'm fine, thanks anyway, how about you?"

"I'm fine too, a few ups and downs, especially downs, anyway, mustn't exaggerate, it goes in cycles."

We'd see each other soon enough. The trade fair is held at the Porte de Versailles at the beginning of June. I hate going to it but it's part of my responsibilities. That's where we all see each other, most of us anyway, every year there are fewer of us. Sometimes we look for someone and they've stopped coming, and each of these disappearances, real or supposed, prepares us in a way. I'd thought about that when I saw him that first time. Where had he drifted in from, to be on Rue d'Amsterdam with a long face like that? Then I called Benjamin, who was leaving for the weekend with Anaïs. He'd repaired his scooter all by himself, like a grown-up. He'd always surprised me like that, I'm barely able to do anything with my hands. Then, on Friday evening, I too left home, the way I used to do sometimes, a few years ago, when I'd go spend the weekend in a country hotel. I met quite a few guys and we'd exchange addresses, but the people you meet there aren't really all that eager to follow through. Most of them are there having illicit weekends with female work colleagues, or else they're trying desperately to live the kind of life they've never really known, or loved. And then, on Sunday evening, they drive back along the A6. The windshield wipers don't wipe out anything, and when they get back home they don't recognize anything, in fact they've never recognized anything. They end up telling themselves their best years are behind them, and sometimes they envy those who have the strength to pull down the curtain completely, like in the book I'd just finished.

"I'm going to take a shower, I'm exhausted."

"Yes, you look it."

I'd read him four times, I think. As a teenager, then in

my first tiny studio apartment, then soon after my divorce, and now. I wouldn't have so many opportunities to read him again in this life. I deleted my profile, and then started to regret it. I hadn't made love in two years. The last time I'd paid a prostitute, a woman who wasn't very young anymore but wasn't ugly, she'd held me in her arms. Is that all, wouldn't you like me to give you a blowjob? No, thanks, no, no, it's all right. She didn't want to rob her customers. She'd give me a discount if I came back, just for that. But no. I wouldn't have been able to, how long had it been? And now Marie had sent me her photos, she'd described the places she often hung out, and in some part of me I didn't want to know more for the moment, she'd already told me too much. I really have to get rid of my computer. Who could I give it to? I knew lots of guys who spent their time inventing lives for themselves, and then, when when they were in over their heads, they found themselves chatting with their Myosotis and they didn't really care anymore, in a way, whether they loved or didn't love anymore. I went home early.

At seven I took a shower and changed for my dinner with Aïcha and Marc-André. He'd be there too, in their apartment in Levallois. I was sure he'd make a point of giving me the translation I'd assigned him at the beginning of the week. Having had a bit of time, I now remembered when the three of us were fifteen. He used to love languages and traveling, I admired him for that. Marco was the only one of us living with both parents. I don't know where it leads sometimes, I'm fed up with remembering, starting to talk to myself without being able to do anything about it. I didn't regret living alone, though, I wasn't desperate. In fact, I felt better than I had before. I went out. There were buds on the trees in Levallois. How things had changed around here. The town that had once had two hundred cafés, the headquarters of Hispano-Suiza, and a whole heap of body shops, was unrecognizable. The Hauts-de-Seine had been colonized by the hard right for about thirty years. It was no longer my world, no longer my home, not for me or for guys like Marc-André, who was obliged because of his job to talk with quite a lot of town councils in the area. Sometimes, I had a strong desire to leave, even though I'd spent my whole life here. But to go where? The trees didn't give a damn, obviously, although they'd been trimmed a bit too much on my street. All the plane trees and chestnut trees near Louise Michel had been punished for their appearance. We had Irish pubs, business restaurants, head offices, a swarm of municipal cops, and surveillance cameras all over the place. Benjamin used to count them on the street on his way to see me when he was in high school. I didn't buy any flowers from the shop near my apartment. I went and had a walk over toward Porte d'Asnières to kill time. For a moment, I had the impression I was being followed, and the guy who was following me was surely a guy like him, a guy like me. Except that when I turned around, there was nobody there.

I bought a bottle of Bordeaux, a very good one, I couldn't remember if Aïcha drank it or not. I've often made errors in tact without realizing it. The trees in the Eiffel neighborhood lining the beltway had also been trimmed. When had they even been planted? Who'd made that decision? I had an old man's thoughts, as Benjamin always said. I had an old man's thoughts, but I was still fed up with it. I walked as far as Sainte-Odile, which is one of the ugliest churches in Paris. I lit a two-euro candle. I don't tell anyone I do that, but I do it all the same, because I'm superstitious. I stood looking at the candle, next to a very beautiful African woman in a denim miniskirt and high-heeled shoes. She was very straight-backed. She was smiling at the flames. Her eyes became bright in the candlelight, I met her gaze. I guess I was disturbing her? We don't always need to look for reasons. Finally, I sat down on a bench near Porte Champerret. The cars were going very slowly where I was, the traffic system was being rerouted. It was good, right then, to have gotten through another week's work and to be going to see my only friend. Tomorrow, I would figure out what to do, spring was on its way. I waited until it was after 8:30 and then walked to their place. I walked quickly, pretending, the way all guys like me do, that I was a man in a hurry, a man who'd never begged for love or anything like that.

He was already there, sitting on the couch in the living room. Aïcha opened the door for me and I don't know why, but when I saw her, I felt a pang in my heart, I don't think she noticed. I don't trust my emotions, because of my solitude, because of my job, because of everything and nothing, both together, all mixed up.

"Ah, there you are!"

She smiled and gave me a hug. We kissed each other on the cheek. Marco took the bottle out of my hands, oh, it's a good one. Jean murmured something I didn't hear. When he went into the kitchen, I noticed that the tail of his shirt was sticking out of his pants, that surprised me coming from him. Aïcha sat down, she's about forty. She's a child psychologist, she does lots of other things too, she's traveled a lot for her work. She's at ease wherever she goes, I think Marco admires her for that too. She knows it, but doesn't exploit it. You get the feeling they've never hidden anything from each other, but I'm not sure. We exchanged a few words and I found myself facing Jean. He gave me his big, slow, tired smile. He stood up, a bit like a fifty-year-old teenager, his hand seemed too long when he held it out to me across the coffee table. Without meaning to, he kept it too long in mine, and then Marco suggested we have a drink.

Their children were all at the movies, together, Marc's and Aïcha's, a reconstructed family. I've often thought about that. I've heard about it at work too. How do people manage that? I've never wanted to talk about it with Marco, whose life, in many respects, is like a criticism of mine, his choices against mine, and yet we're friends. Maybe that's part of the reason we're friends. Jean wasn't talking much, as if he had to learn how to talk all over again. I remembered that feeling that you've forgotten how to say things, it had happened to me between my divorce and being hired by the company where I'm still working today, but with him there was something else. Every once in a while, Aïcha glanced at the balcony. She said she wanted Marco to put up a hammock there, so that they could take afternoon naps when the weather was fine. He'd always tell her it was impossible. She'd ask why. They always got very heated about this hammock business. Jean perked up a bit on the subject, he'd spent a lot of time in northern Europe, and in Germany. He'd been on the road in the old days. After a while, his description of a trip to Norway got lost in limbo, and I couldn't help meeting Marc-André's amused gaze, we both felt like laughing, the way we had before. How slow he was these days.

Aïcha doesn't usually talk much. But she follows everything, commenting on it with a nod or a shake of the head, it's as if she knows hundreds of ways to do that. Marc-André is lucky to have found her, at an age when it was still possible to change. I tell myself that sometimes, when I'm alone and indulge in the jealousy of regrets. Then I'm no longer so sure, because even knowing his happiness, it seems too good for me. Since I've been living alone, I've often been ashamed of who I am, as if I've been spending too much time with myself. And yet I'm also part of guys like him, in a sense. Except that I have a job, so I don't have time these days to show my cracks, or let them open up even more. He was talking in an even tone, he seemed to be happy that evening. Aïcha put on some music, old stuff we all liked, I still know three albums by Leonard Cohen by heart, we sat down on the couch. After a while, the telephone rang.

"Excuse me," she murmured.

Marco followed her with his eyes until she closed the door of their bedroom behind her. He'd sometimes talked to me about this. Aïcha's mother could spend hours on the phone and, to his wife, it was unthinkable to say stop, I'm in a hurry, I'll call you back, she couldn't do that. It scared him every time, although he couldn't explain it. Was he afraid that she'd leave one day after hanging up? He poured some more wine, there was much more to this phone business than just the phone. Once, when I'd told him that, he'd shrugged, he'd looked at me with those dark, feverish eyes of his, which he's always had since we've known each other.

"That's it, it's her mother," he said.

He didn't seem to realize. He'd resumed his place at the end of the big couch in the corner of the room. They'd bought that couch for a ridiculously high price, I'd helped him to transport it in a rented Peugeot J7. He'd been pleased to do it with me. Aïcha spoke three languages in addition to ours, more beautifully than us, because it was Lebanese French that she spoke.

"By the way," Marco said, looking at Jean, "I think I have something for you. Anyway, we can always try, the guy knows all about you."

His eyes shone for a brief moment, while Marco explained to him what the work consisted of. Yes, they'd already checked his résumé.

"Do you think I'll be able to do it?"

Yes, it was right up his alley. He'd spent ten years with Linotier, hadn't he? Yes, until they closed following the

buyback. The salary wasn't what he might reasonably expect, obviously. But it was a question of take it or leave it.
I stopped myself from smiling, all the time Marco was explaining the job to him with his usual brusqueness, which
is nothing like the fake kindness I sometimes assume in
order to do nothing. Jean was listening the way you listen to a story that's somehow too mysterious to be really
interesting. He nodded from time to time. If I'd been in
Marc-André's place, it would have irritated me. I decided
not to mention the translation. He might have felt un-
comfortable being indebted to both of us the same time,
while Aïcha was talking to her mother in Beirut, shut up
in their bedroom after eleven at night. Toward the end,
he stammered that he didn't know what to say, but Marc-
André was only interested, so to speak, in the door of the
bedroom, with his dark eyes.

"Is everything all right, Marco?"

After a while, as if he couldn't hold out any longer,
he excused himself. When he came back, he was looking
straight ahead of him at the window to the balcony, trying
to put on a bold front, but he seemed hurt.

When Aïcha rejoined us, the embarrassment faded rapidly. It was a nice evening. We celebrated the news,
even though we were counting our chickens before they
hatched. That expression made me laugh, I must have
been a little drunk, and when they asked me why, I said it
was a strange phrase, why should people bother to count
chickens anyway? I'd also had too much aperitif, before
that. Aïcha laughed at my joke, yes, she said, why should
people count chickens? And how about you, how are
things with you? We were both in the middle of putting
our plates in the dishwasher. How's Benjamin? She lit a
cigarette.

"He's fine."

"Do you have anyone right now?"

I felt myself blush like a young man for the second time that evening. I said no, a few dates, you know how it is, it isn't so easy to find love. She held out her hand.

"You'll find her one day, when you've stopped looking!"

Her eyes were smiling. We both laughed together, in the kitchen.

As we got out of the elevator downstairs, we ran into their children coming back from the movies. Marc-André's daughter kissed me on the cheek, and then they took the stairs. We were both on the street now. He was still carrying his case.

He pointed. "Right, I'm going to Porte de Champerret. There's a night bus that goes to La Garenne-Colombes."

I suggested walking with him part of the way because I didn't feel like going straight home. We didn't talk much.

"Nice evening, wasn't it?"

"Yes, it was."

By the way, he hadn't yet finished the translation. I told him not to worry, if he could give it to me by the end of the following week, it'd be fine. It was better to take too much time than too little, if he wanted it to be well received. We walked like two shadows, his empty case between the two of us. We were a long way from all those years together, when it came down to it. But anyway, we really had had a nice evening. He might have a job, at his age he hadn't expected that. We sat down on a bench in the big bus station at Porte Champerret. A lot of young people, with their headphones in their ears or their cell phones on, a few couples too. A lot of guys like him and me who didn't have cars. They'd be going a long way, when the night bus finally arrived. He was pleased. He told me in a low voice that, more than once, he'd thought to end it all, because he couldn't bear not having anything to do, day after day, night after night. I let him speak without interrupting him. What do you say to someone who confides his fears in you, his desire to end it all, when you yourself don't know? Another guy like me, that's what you are, my brother. Who'd want to abandon his brother, or refuse to hear him? We'd meet again soon.

Life resumed its course. I called Marie, who I definitely couldn't get out of my head. We met on Tuesday evening near Chaussée d'Antin. We went to a café she knew, she struck me as pretty right from the start, I think. She was smiling at me, I hadn't been very sure I'd recognize her. But in the end, I did. She really was the age she'd told me, and so was I. We sat down, surrounded by a whole bunch of women who worked in the big department stores, she spent a lot of time in this neighborhood. I used to go there too, as a child, with my mother, but in those days it hadn't yet been rebuilt. The area around Passage du Havre and Chaussée d'Antin had been part of the magic of the world for me. It was also here that I'd known a woman for the first time, in the biblical sense, to use Marc-André's phrase. He went with me to the place where I'd spotted her on the sidewalk several Sundays running, on Rue de Mogador. Marie ordered tea. She was a nurse. Right now, she was working for a local organization that helped people with HIV, she'd traveled a lot before that. She'd worked for various humanitarian organizations, she'd kind of drifted into it. She was pleased she'd been away so long and had come back after it all. It had only been two years. Time passes, doesn't it?

Her eyes were very black, her gaze slightly sardonic, I thought. On several occasions, I had the impression she was sizing me up, so after a while I actually asked her, is there something wrong with me? Is that it? She seemed surprised at first. Then she softened a little, in any case it was still too early to love, let alone to let myself be loved,

I needed time. I didn't tell her that, of course, I didn't say anything about the subject.

"You aren't very talkative, tell me something."

"Oh, really?"

So I made an effort, as if I had to learn all over again, although I didn't have time to learn all over again, but anyway. She had a couple of tickets for the theater, by the way, a friend of hers had begged off at the last moment, how does that grab you? Do you know it? No, I said, I've only seen the posters in the metro, but on the other hand I do know the story of the guy who's always asking if he can pull down the curtain, and in the end nobody minds if he draws a veil over who he was, and also over his own life. He'd end his life alone. I was making a real hash of this first date, I just wasn't used to it, I think that's what it was. Fortunately, Marie loved books, she bought lots of them. Since she'd come back from Mali, she'd been making up for lost time. We talked for a good hour, in the end.

I paid for our drinks and she got up while I was doing that and went downstairs to the toilet, I watched her, she was well dressed, in black with a white blouse. Her hair was black too. She wore lots of bracelets. Would it have been hard to say what she did for a living? She looked a lot like her photo on the website. Would we see each other again? I'd had enough of all those dates that never lead to anything, as if after a while, for guys like me, there's no tomorrow. I waited for her outside, on the sidewalk. The stores were open, the weather wasn't really nice yet, but all the same. It had taken me so many years to forget that I think, in the end, I wasn't sure anymore what it was I wanted to forget. I looked at the customers in the café. The waiters, the high school kids, you often saw them laughing and smiling, how to take my place among them again? I wanted to make love with Marie. I remember very well how much I wanted that, standing there on the side-walk, on Chaussée d'Antin. Without doing it deliberately, I looked at myself in the mirror at the end of the room, wondering if it was still possible for a woman to want to wake up in bed with a guy like me the following morning. How are you? Did you sleep well? Yes, how about you? Tea or coffee? For years and years. I had to remember not to let myself go when I was with her. When she came back, I saw she'd taken the time to touch up her lipstick. I was pleased about that, though I couldn't quite say why. We talked a little more, smiling at each other, and at the corner of Rue du Havre, after all those hours talking online, I felt like kissing her.

"You certainly don't waste any time."

"There isn't much of it, Marie."

She looked at me for a long time without replying. Then she said yes, that's true. Her eyes clouded over a little at that moment. We'll see later, shall we? Then she said goodbye, lovely to have met you, if you can't make the theater, let me know. It was for that Friday evening. I watched her walk away, one woman among other women on her way to the Chaussée d'Antin station. I told myself she wouldn't turn around, and she didn't. In the metro I also told myself the game wasn't over yet, of course it wasn't. Among all those people going in and out of the metro, there had to be quite a few guys like me, just as there were among the people I met at work. We had to have a stroke of luck, another woman, someone to cling to ... I took the metro to go home, I felt like calling her. I'd been rough, but she hadn't seemed all that surprised. I thought of calling Benjamin instead, but I didn't want to bother him too much. He'd always liked repairing things. When he was small he'd have liked to repair his parents' divorce, he'd never be able to repair everything, obviously. I got out at Louise Michel.

He was at the metro exit. When I saw him, he was looking at the name of the street on the corner, his body a bit
lopsided, as if he'd had to lean back to see the sign. He
turned right in the direction of my place. I wanted to be
alone, I was thinking about Marie, about all those weeks
of empty words, those confidences we'd shared with each
other, none of that had anything to do with him. When he
got to my street, he leaned back again to see the sign on
the wall at the corner. That made me smile, he was making
it clear what he was looking for, as if he might risk arrest if
he didn't. He took a big envelope from his case, he'd surely
come to drop off the work I'd given him. Marc-André had
told me they'd cut off his phone, after too many unpaid
bills. He'd offered him money so that he could pay, but
he'd refused. I stood there hidden by part of a wall, and
then, after he'd deposited the envelope, I decided to follow
him, like a fool playing a foolish game. We walked some
distance from each other, toward Porte de Champerret.
We passed the bench where we'd sat after the evening at
Marco's and talked while waiting for the night bus.

He was walking quickly, a lot quicker than me, as if he was
always in a hurry. Sometimes that's the way people walk
when they're dying, that was the impression I had, but I
always have a lot of thoughts that don't mean anything at
all, so anyway. He was about to get on his bus when he
turned around, I was maybe about a hundred feet away,
on the other side of Place du Général Pershing. I don't
know if he saw me. He got on his bus, he was going back
to the far end of the Hauts-de-Seine, where he and Marc-
André and I had spent our childhood. Young people,
people alone. People still with earphones in their ears and
free newspapers in their hands. The news often seems old
and out of date at seven in the morning, even though the
paper's new. Maybe that's why they give it to us for free
these days? I walked toward the bus, I didn't want him to

think I'd seen him without even deigning to make a sign. I couldn't even call him about the translation, he'd told me he'd be finished soon, and he was enjoying getting back into the swing of things, the bus left. I turned back, some nice things had happened in my life today, I'd met Marie. I picked up the envelope when I got home, he had specially bought one of those expandable envelopes and marked the flap with a cross. I put it down on the coffee table and tidied up the place a little. Marie must be home by now. I went on the website and kept going back to the screen to see if she was online, because I wanted to say thank you, and above all to tell her all the things that had crossed my mind beforehand and afterwards, but not at the time. Why not call her? It was better to wait. I called Benjamin, he was fine, Anaïs was spending a few days at her mother's, he'd be happy to drop by.

"Great, you're coming, then? Be careful on the road."

I switched off the computer and left a message on Marie's answering machine, I waited a while, then said it was really nice to meet you, something dumb like that, thanks for this afternoon. See you soon. Do you mind if I pull down the curtain? No, go ahead, why not?

My son and I wanted to go to the pizzeria, but in the end we went to Place Voltaire. My head was too big for Anaïs's helmet. What was that Italian movie where a guy visited Rome on a scooter, with the music of Keith Jarrett over images of the city as he rode through it? I asked Benjamin when we came to a red light. Nanni Moretti! Oh yes, that's right. We reached the couscous place on the other side of the Seine, at Asnières. We were almost alone in the restaurant. It wasn't yet nine in the evening. We had the Royale, which isn't expensive. It was a place I used to go, occasionally on my own just to treat myself, I know the guy who runs it, from having been so often. Since my divorce, the Kabyle man and I had both aged, there were times now when he wasn't there. But whenever we saw each other, we always shook hands, how's the family? Fine, and yours? And I'd never leave the restaurant without saying goodbye, even if I had to go through the kitchens, where the radio was always playing with the volume way down. Benjamin was exhausted. He had exams and he was working with some friends on a complicated project. I tried to follow his explanations, but I could hardly understand a word of what he told me. I'd already heard so many stories like that, it was something he'd wanted to do since the age of ten or eleven. And how's your life these days? His eyes are very bright, sometimes he's like, here's the answer, what was the question? He was fine. Everything was really fine. His mother always said you never know with him, but I didn't find that. We finished the couscous, I thought it was very good, and we had quite a bit of time after that to do what both of us liked the most, we looked around the room without saying anything. It was pretty much always the same around here, guys on their own, regulars from Place Voltaire and the surrounding area. I really had to buy a scooter so that I could get to the places I liked more easily. We had a mint tea with pine nuts. We smoked, and I realized that a day like this, an evening like this too, like a whole lot of other evenings really, shouldn't be forgotten. I was quite emotional about it. I asked him are you coming, shall we go? Ben didn't ask for his change. It was almost a month since we'd last seen each other in the flesh, Anaïs was always telling him to invite me over for dinner, but most of the time he was snowed under with his research in the lab. The Kabyle man wasn't there. Say hello to Slimane for me. No problem, see you soon!

We rode along the Seine. It was the route I took every day when I was a teenager, on my moped, with Marco and Jean and a whole bunch of other guys I'd stopped seeing.

After a while, I tapped him on the shoulder. Step on the gas! He didn't seem to understand, but we did eighty on the section of the road running alongside the river over toward Tour Bellini. Finally he came out and drove nice and gently in the opposite direction, toward Pont de Levallois. I wanted to give my son a hug, but instead we just talked about the following week. We turned left, in the direction of Louise Michel, and I felt very happy and very old at the same time, that evening. I didn't feel like going to bed, I wouldn't be able to sleep.

"Are you coming up?"

"No, I'm going home, I'm exhausted. So long, call me!"

She hadn't left any message on the answering machine. I didn't turn on the computer. I was pleased that I didn't, who could I say that to? The best thing would still have been not to have to say it at all, not to want to talk to another guy like me. I still had the music from the *Köln Concert* by Keith Jarrett in my head and the images from the movie by Nanni Moretti, that movie didn't mean much to Benjamin. Barely a childhood memory.

He'd taped a floppy disk onto a sheet of cardboard. I read a few passages, a complicated transfer contract, it made my mind go numb, it was very boring, I went to bed. I skimmed through the pages. It seemed OK to me. He hadn't given me any invoice. Surely that was the most important thing? I'd had a good day. I tried to revisit Rome in my sleep, to go all the way to Ostia, but I wasn't very successful. That was my first trip when I was eighteen, Marco and his girlfriend, the girl who would become my wife, and me. I decided I couldn't wait any longer, I was going to buy myself a scooter. I'd wanted one for a long time. And besides, for a guy like me, who almost never goes on vacation, I could go for rides in my suburb, my whole life was in that area. I dreamed about someone behind me, I had her hair on my neck, she was holding me very tight. I even remembered her perfume. Who was it? I didn't have many dreams like that these days. When I woke up it was after eight.

3

I saw Marie twice the following week. She often
had things to do near the Opéra, so we ended up meeting
in that area. We quickly got used to each other, I think. I
had the impression she was making an effort. Sometimes
she seemed to be looking for something in my eyes, a
trace of what, I wondered? I didn't know the name of it.
Had I ever known it? Nobody could tell me. I liked those
first dates, we kissed, we laughed like kids. She liked it
too, the old teenager in the photo, anyone would think
that was me. In any case, I made some good resolutions,
even though for several years I've been trying to avoid
mirrors as if they were the ones cheating. I'd finished the
book, put the computer back in its place, on the desk in
my office, not on the coffee table in the living room. I
don't remember when I called him about his invoice, I
hadn't received it. He replied in a flat voice, exactly the
voice you'd expect from the lost guy I'd met a few weeks
earlier, that he didn't pay much attention to things like
that. I'd spoken with Marco on the phone, he was snowed
under with work. All the same he'd taken the time to set
up a meeting for him, now it was in his hands.

"How's Antoine?"

He hadn't been to see him, usually he went every week.

"I haven't heard from him. Listen, I'm in a hurry, see
you soon."

The weather was nice now, people went out with colorful umbrellas, there were showers almost every day. On those days, it was as if people were off to discover the world in the morning, and then, how beautiful the world is, when they're on their lunch break. As soon as I got his invoice, I took it to accounts myself to make sure he'd be paid quickly. I insisted, he'd done us a great service, I called him to tell him. It looked like there might be a storm, the windows in my apartment were open. He picked up after the second ring, as if he'd been waiting all day by the phone, and in his case that wasn't just a figure of speech. Yes, he'd spoken with Marco. He'd tell me if he had the slightest problem. When I hung up, I felt like shaking him from afar. But after all, who was I to get irritated by his attitude? He didn't always seem to be all there, that was all. I felt very tired, I remember. I closed the windows. I looked at myself in the closet mirror, full face, then profile, then three-quarters, that belly I couldn't completely pull in, because I was fifty-four. I felt sorry about how things had gone for him, but that was it. He might have a job again thanks to Marc-André's intervention. On Friday night, I took Marie out to dinner, I'd gone home beforehand to take a shower and change. I'd hesitated like a young man, she didn't like guys from offices dressed like penguins. So I was in a real fix. I put on a pair of jeans and looked at myself in the closet mirror. I could have spent three whole days of my life looking at myself in the closet mirror, trying to decide if it was OK, or if it wasn't OK, and it still wouldn't have given me the right answer.

We talked for a long time, she and I. We had time to drink a bottle and I saw her home. She lived not far from Brochant, in a little three-room apartment she'd had for a long time. She'd paid next to nothing for it at the time. Sometimes she seemed lost in thought. I looked at her without knowing. We made love, we'd both been wanting it for a long time, since the e-mails and the last few weeks. We'd simply waited a while, we'd needed time. Do you mind if I switch off the light? We did it gently, for a long time, I didn't have any difficulty in getting an erection. I liked the way we both lay there afterwards, without moving, holding each other tight. There was more noise at her place than in my building in Levallois, and besides, it was Saturday. I went to buy some croissants from the bakery on the corner. When I went back upstairs, Marie was already dressed, I didn't know what to expect.

"Are you OK? I've brought some croissants."

"Yes, I'm fine, how about you?"

We kept looking at each other, on the sly, I'd say. We sometimes smiled at each other without saying anything.

"Marie, are you sure you're OK?"

"Yes, I'm fine. Would you like tea or coffee?"

She had to go to work in the afternoon, she was the nurse on duty. She wanted to be alone for a while before that, we'll speak on the phone tonight, OK? I felt pleased to be going home, I went down the boulevard as far as Porte de Clichy. I knew the area quite well, I looked at the people curiously, eyes wide open. I walked to the Cité des Fleurs, I'd spent some time not far from there in the '80s in connection with a job, it was a private street, with houses on either side, a well-preserved place, with birds in the trees and very clear clouds in the blue sky. Marie. I had no regrets this time. Maybe in the life of a guy like me, there was still room for a few good years? I hadn't had my fair share, to be honest. I'd screwed up without realizing it. I crossed the Maréchaux and found myself in Clichy, after the Lycée Balzac, the service stations, and the entrance ramp to the northern beltway. For almost a quarter of a mile, there are Arab shops and used car lots, and then, as if I was a prince or something, I raised my hand to hail a passing taxi. It took me home in less than ten minutes and

I was happy about all that. Another life. Again. I only had to wait until tonight to talk to her. Another life. For free. Yet another life. It's a gift. She often looked worried, I thought. I wondered why. After all, she was very popular. I went to the library in Levallois, and then I changed my mind, I decided I'd rather buy F. Scott Fitzgerald's other books. I did a bit of shopping at the Monoprix near the town hall, surrounded by other guys like me. I went back home and waited for her to call me.

· · ·

"I know almost nothing about him," I said to Marco.

We were both sitting in his living room, the picture window wide open at the end of April. It was as if the trees had spread the word, the ones beside the Seine seemed incredibly green, as if they weren't yet used to it. I remembered how when my father, who I hadn't known very well, died, I was twenty-four at the time, the sun came through a stained glass window in the transept of the church of Notre Dame de la Croix in Ménilmontant and hit my forehead.

"I remember a bit," Marco replied. "Don't you remember how friendly he was to us?"

"Yes, it's true."

We were sitting side by side, with the sun facing us. He told me you couldn't see anything when the sun shone, that he'd been wanting to put in blinds for a long time, but his sadness had nothing to do with that, when it came down to it.

"What time are we supposed to be there, shall we go?"

"We have time, you've already asked me twice," he said.

We drank another coffee.

"I hadn't seen him for about a year, I think. I didn't

know it was so serious, what he had."

"He never said, he didn't want anybody to know," Marc-André murmured. "He didn't want it, you know. Did you tell the people in Asnières?"

"Yes, everybody I could remember."

We talked some more about guys, old friends we'd lost touch with, after a while it became painful to live with too many of these memories, it's age, Marco said. And time. You can't do anything against time. Finally we left for the ceremony.

Jean hadn't arrived yet. He'd found a little job thanks to Marc-André. We went along a row of seats that wasn't too far back. A woman in front, much younger than him, I wondered if it could be his wife, or else his sister. He had a daughter the same age as Benjamin, Élise, I think, I saw her when I went for a meal at his house, many years earlier. She had very white skin, like him, her tears were flowing, by themselves, should I kiss her and give her my condolences? There were also a few guys from the last place where he'd worked, I recognized some of them from the branch I'd been fired from nearly ten years ago. I couldn't put names to the faces. Sometimes it's the other way around, Marc-André and I had talked about that. Sometimes you search for a face to match the name.

Marie wouldn't be at my place in the evening, and I probably wouldn't be going to Brochant, unless during our phone call I felt like she was asking me to, without saying anything, the way she did most of the time. I'd figure it out without wanting to, already. I don't like that word: already. It was cold in the church, April never comes in churches. Jean arrived five minutes after us, which let the light in through the left door, I turned around in the direction of the noise. He was moving forward on tiptoe, as if, even in the anonymity of a funeral, he didn't want to disturb anyone. The priest started droning on about this guy, who'd never even set foot in a church, I turned to Marco and saw that he was crying and making no attempt to hide it. We took each other's hands, I wanted to wait outside for the priest to finish his stupid speech. But actually, no, he was looking around, with his blue eyes and his weary air, as if he was on a visit somewhere. There weren't thirty people in all. Maybe other people would be coming to the cemetery, I held out that hope for him, and for all the guys like him, I made a few promises to myself at that moment. We stood in line behind, and waited for the family to pass. He ended up in front of me, he said something I didn't hear. I approached in turn and put my hand on the coffin, that was the way it was now, we saw each other in church, I didn't like to think about it.

I went to wait for Marco, the family lined up in front, his wife, his daughter, it was definitely them. We went out, there were trees all around the square, Marc-André had only half an hour, I didn't have much longer, in the end we wouldn't be going to the cemetery. Jean joined us. All the time that the guys were putting the coffin in the hearse, he stayed quite close to them, watching with a stunned air, as if he'd never seen anybody doing that before, which I thought was unbelievable, and then he came toward us. Marco was smoking a cigarette on a bench at the side of the square. Later in the day, I remembered lots of other squares with little parks in them, like the one where I used to take Benjamin when he was little, Square Max de Nansouty in Asnières. One day, dulled by alcohol and pills, I decided to check who he was. I'd always assumed he was a great explorer. He was a mechanic, I think. Then Marco stepped away to make a phone call. He had to call Aïcha. When he hung up he looked at his watch.

"We could go for a drink if you like. Do you have time?"

We set off in search of the nearest bar. Jean placed himself between Marc-André and me, and although he walked too slowly, he managed to keep up with us. We talked a little about him, it had happened very suddenly, maybe he hadn't suffered? Jean was nodding his head, vaguely interested, he was looking around him without touching his coffee. I saw something in him again that I'd been aware of since our schooldays, the way he had of hearing you without seeming to, like children you scold and who wait patiently for you to finish before going off to play. He didn't seem any more moved than that.

"Oh, yes," he said, "it happens."

"What do you mean, it happens?" I asked him.

Marc-André and I looked at each other, I think I even felt like laughing at that moment, but he insisted, it was one of those things that happened.

"You remember Nazim?"

Yes, of course, why? He told us that Nazim had died within two days, he'd climbed on a stool to change a light bulb and felt bad, and that was it, he'd had a quadruple bypass, but it was no use. He died two days later. Marco lit another cigarette, he held out the pack to us, gradually resuming the attitude he'd always had since our teenage years, a kind of friendly gang leader, always ready with a joke, but he was a lot more than that for me. I'd known that ever since my separation and those years of solitude, and also, as he'd pointed out to me, as only he could because I probably wouldn't have accepted it from anyone else, those years of suspicion toward women, I'd had to rid myself of that in order to carry on, to hope that I could get something going again. He asked him, but how do you know that? Jean put on that smart-ass look of his, how do I know? I just know. Nazim had lived in Bois-Colombes, right next to the station, he had a little painting and decorating business, he'd gone to see him for a bit of moonlighting, after two years without a job.

"By the way," we asked him, "how's your job going?"

He looked at us for a long time, just as he had looked at the coffin on its way to the hearse, that's the impression I had, it's OK, he murmured, everything's fine, thanks. Thanks, he said again to Marc-André, in a flat voice, but in fact we'd already changed the subject, we'd probably be in touch during the week. Maybe we'd spend an hour together, maybe go have a meal, to say what we'd felt about this.

For some years now, what with all the people we knew who'd left us, the women who'd haunted our dreams, the women we'd loved in our suburb who'd later suffered cancer or depression, we'd had very few opportunities to talk to each other. When it came down to it, you had only the memory of that absence in front of your eyes, when night falls. He insisted on paying for the coffees, we said thanks, that's nice of you. He took a ten-euro bill from his pocket, as if it was parchment. He handed it to the waitress. Marco and I looked at each other, she gave him his change. He put it in his wallet with slow, measured gestures, and the three of us left.

"Now's maybe not the time," he said to us in a flat voice in the sunshine, "but I'd like to invite the two of you over for dinner."

Marco smiled, yes, but when? He turned to me, sure that I'd be pleased. He looked toward the corner of the street. Right at the end, at the intersection with Boulevard Jules Ferry, where the trees had also been trimmed too close, only the big branches were left, and it was sad to look at them. It would stay sad all spring, for a few years. He seemed to think slowly, slowly like the long-term unemployed person he'd been these last few years.

"One day next week?"

Marco nodded and took out his personal organizer, let's see. I could make it on Friday the 17th, how about you?

Yes, that suits me fine. Marie and I had settled on two nights a week, we were also going to spend some weekends together, when the weather got better. We'd talked about it, but I didn't yet know when. All right then, he said to us. And suddenly, his face seemed to brighten up, what ordeals had he been through in all those years? He held out his hand. He almost dumped us there, Marco and me, just outside the metro station.

"He really has turned a little strange, hasn't he?" Marc-André said. "Was he always like that?"

We almost laughed again.

"At least he's got a job now."

Marco nodded. "Well, they've extended his trial period. I had a call from Langinieux. I don't know if he'll be suitable."

"Oh, really?"

He looked at his watch. We sat down again, on another bench; there was a dark sun in the depths of the shop windows, noises and shadows. We could have spent days on end on benches, him and me. It wasn't so bad, when it came down to it. We said goodbye on the metro platform. Each of us got into his own subway car. He had to stay at the rear of the train in order to change at Gare Saint-Lazare. Me at the opposite end. Speak on the phone? Yes, bye! These days, I think about him almost every day. Sometimes we call each other at the same moment, and when that happens, he really is a guy like me, and me like him.

Time started up again. Benjamin invited me the following evening. There was lots of work at the office, they'd finished the balance sheets, so people were staying later, not that this changed the situation in any way. I dropped by the scooter store in Clichy-Levallois, they had some nice ones, I thought, I spent a while there. Let me know if you have any questions. The assistant was Ben's age, or not far off. Sometimes, in all those years, it had been my ex-wife I carried behind me in my dreams, and my mother too, whom I hadn't seen for a long time. Once, though, she took me gently in her arms at a red light. She was giving me the love that had always been denied me in my childhood, but, when the lights changed and I turned to look at her, she'd already disappeared ... Benjamin was fine and so was Anaïs. They were becoming more and more visible, more and more apparent as a couple. I hadn't talked with her very much, but we hadn't been distant either. I kept talking about the scooter, they looked at each other two or three times, wondering what's gotten into him? Benjamin was trying to keep a straight face. By the way, he had a job offer from a big lab in Zurich, it was well paid, much more than he could make here. Anaïs was quite pleased, although it wasn't convenient for her. I listened without saying anything. But when I was leaving, he told me not to worry, they weren't going forever! I didn't understand right away. Later I did, but it was too late by then, near the metro station, where I was going to take my train home and it wouldn't embarrass anybody if I cried, for no reason, just like that.

After all these years, he was still afraid to leave me on my own. The Seine was very full near the railroad bridge, it was a little oily, the lights spread out with the current, the lights from the towers of La Défense and the lights of the cars driving along the banks. My son. My ex-wife. Marco and the other guys like me. My mother so long ago, my father whom I'd barely known, which was probably why I could put him on my list. I'd enjoyed the evening, having dinner with them, knowing that he was going to leave but that Anaïs wanted to go with him and also knowing that around midnight that night, Marie would be coming back from the theater. She and her girlfriends had a subscription, I'd give her a call. We'd chat as long as we needed to, five minutes or an hour, I don't know. It was good anyway. Guys like me don't have any more to say to those who don't really want to listen. But with those who are like them, they can talk for hours, they could just as easily keep quiet, I think. Anyway, it didn't matter. Then the platform, in the direction of Pont de Levallois.

Marie hadn't liked the play. She told me about her day. I remember where I was, near the glass doors leading into the living room. She wasn't far from my place, as the crow flies. After Porte de Champerret, you had to turn left, it wasn't so far. I bit my lips, I didn't tell her about the funeral. I hadn't wanted to tell her about the scooter, she'd said, oh yes, it's a good idea, but it was no concern of hers. We hadn't argued yet, maybe those hours on end behind computer screens had taught us more about each other than I imagined, but sometimes I thought she was on the verge of blowing a fuse. She told me off for being too attached to my past, my previous life, my friends, my years of marriage, I hadn't gotten over it. I didn't reply. What could I have found to tell her off about? Do you mind if I pull down the curtain? She read parts of me like a book, but after all, why not? Good night, Marie, and then I hung up. I'd also have to buy a scooter if I had another disappointment in love. That evening, I spent quite a lot of time on the computer, bicycle websites, I didn't know which one to choose. I went back to the dating website after a while, she was online, which shocked me. I could have called her and asked her why? Friends, strangers like you. Life, often, finds it hard to be like us. I had his wife and daughter in my eyes that night. It was two in the morning, I went and took a shower. I barely recognized my face, who had I been before? It wouldn't do me any harm to spend the evening at home the following day. I was exhausted. Worry lines that make you look like a thinker were one thing, but why those crow's feet at the corners of the eyes and those first brown patches on the backs of my hands, yes, why?

...

"Well," Marc-André said. "I didn't know it was here. Did you remember?"

I wasn't sure. Jean lived in one of the few places in La Garenne-Colombes that hadn't yet changed, which meant it looked pretty decrepit. If you turned around, you couldn't recognize the neighborhood at all, from there to Place de Belgique. We looked at each other and smiled. Jean had called me again the previous evening, this invitation seemed to be really important to him. I didn't know what to expect. I was pleased to be going there, there are hundreds of pointless evenings in a life, this one though was different, plus to be going back to La Garenne-Colombes, which had been part of me since my teenage years. The first things I saw, entering his apartment, were the second-hand furniture and the linoleum in the kitchen, as if nothing had changed since our childhood. He had his weary look, he'd just taken a shower, that's the impression I had. He shook our hands really firmly, like one of those salesmen who want to impress you and strike the fear of God into you without showing it.

He couldn't stop thanking us, how nice of us to come, and it would have become embarrassing if we'd kept saying no, what was embarrassing was that we hadn't yet had anything to drink. It was the end of April now. He lived on the ground floor facing the courtyard. He couldn't stay there, it was a short-term lease. Through the half-open window a cat came and looked at us, and although he was carrying the ice tray he couldn't stop himself from approaching the cat.

"He's been coming to see me every day since I've been living here."

The three of us sat down, he took the stool. He looked at us, drinking the pastis.

"How long have you been living here?"

He looked as if he was counting before answering. Nearly six months. It had belonged to his uncle. Did we remember him? He sometimes came to the lodge in Asnières, don't you remember? I saw Marco make an effort to remember, but no, he didn't, even though he too spent more and more time remembering, trying and sometimes really remembering things. We said no. I thought it might be best to quickly change the subject, but he was already launched. He'd been through three and a half years of hell. It was his family that had supported him in the last year, he hadn't wanted to go on welfare, it was thanks to them that he'd rented this apartment.

"It's not bad here, anyway," we told him. He wanted to show us everything. We all went out into the inner courtyard, there were two children's bikes and a little orange tent, which belonged to the kids opposite. He'd never had children. He told us that even more slowly, actually there were a lot of things he hadn't had in this life. Once or twice, that evening, I laughed very loudly, I wasn't really laughing at him, because when it came down to it he was like me, except that our lives weren't similar anymore. We went back into the room, he poured us some more pastis. He'd put small plates inside larger ones, he served a big mixed salad, I realized what it meant to him. When was the last time he'd had guests? And, although it was impossible to ask him, when was the last time he'd had a woman here? So we were really there for him, he kept looking at us, there were moments of silence between the salad and the chicken. Then he started talking. He really didn't know anymore when his troubles had started. When we were together in high school? Or even before? He'd never asked himself the question. After a while, he said to us, guys like him have to learn everything over again, and nobody gives them a hand, they can't. This wasn't going to be much fun, I thought, Marc-André lit a cigarette, so I did too, in memory of the good old days, so to speak, he hadn't had any of those either, good old days, but to be honest, he didn't give a damn.

The first thing he always did when he got up in the morning was to open the window and let the cat in and give it a little milk. From the morning onwards, he'd think of all those distant years, those years outside, in the unlikeliest places, oh really? He gave us that slow smile, yes, a place here, a room there, not far from here, but he would never have suspected their existence, like when you see guys sleeping under the entrance ramps to the northern beltway, around La Chapelle, Clichy too. We sat down on the sofa bed, he was sorry, he hadn't made any dessert. He wasn't really good at desserts yet. We talked, when it came down to it things hadn't been too bad for him, did he have any music at least? He looked around, he had some old LPs and also a few DVDs of movies, since he'd started in his new job he'd been buying *Le Monde*, they sold DVDs as a supplement on the weekends, he got them in the hopes of buying a player one day. We smiled. When he'd had his troubles, video cassettes were still the thing, how long ago was that anyway, how long? We didn't ask him the question. So, to cheer himself up, he suggested some more pastis, with a greedy air, he himself had never taken to drink during his bad years, but he knew guys, guys who weren't like him for that very reason, except that to be honest he could have. You never know where the wind takes you, or what can happen to you. After a while, Marc-André couldn't help smiling. The two of us were sitting on the sofa bed and he on a second-hand chair, he leaned toward us: how about you two? We didn't know what to say, obviously. Marco lit another cigarette.

"What can I say? Things are OK for me. Yes, they're OK. I haven't had all these money problems like you."

He nodded. "It won't happen to you, I'm sure of that, you're not the kind."

Fortunately, the cat from the courtyard distracted our attention, it came in through the window and strolled between our legs. We sat there, watching the cat.

We left just after midnight. He left us on the sidewalk outside his building, both hands in his pockets, standing very straight. Marco had his car with him and we went back together, going through Courbevoie, through places we'd known forever and which I really couldn't recognize anymore in spite of everything. I would never have suspected ... Neither would I, I said. Neither would I.

"Did you notice how he carefully avoided talking about his job today?"

We were driving along the riverbank now, no need to go that way, but after all why not?

"By the way," I said, "I'm going to buy a scooter."

"Is that so?"

We slowed down on the Pont de Levallois.

"Why didn't he talk about his job, do you know?"

"It isn't going well ... I talked to the guy I know, they don't want to keep him on."

"Really?"

For years, there had been cobblestones along here. The road had been restored and enlarged, but in places there were still cobblestones on the road to Asnières.

"He's always late, he gets into arguments, he has a nasty temper."

We didn't say anything more after that. Marco dropped me off outside my building. I didn't have any messages on the answering machine. I drank a large glass of water. I took a couple of aspirin because of all the pastis, I should have been more careful. If I'd dared I would have called Benjamin, but it was far too late. So I went to bed.

I hadn't heard much from Marie lately. We were a little angry with each other, especially her, I think. How have you lived all these years, why don't you go back to your wife? She blamed me for not telling her these things, it was the first time in a very long time that I'd been asked that question, I hadn't been able to answer her immediately. She drove in the nail: it's as if you haven't gotten over her, is that it? We were at her place, in Brochant, we'd actually had a nice evening. We were still trying to please each other, and perhaps to love each other, it was a gift when it came down to it, for a guy like me, but it was that thing about not getting over my wife that set me off. Why had her saying that gotten me so riled up?

"She's the mother of my son, we haven't spoken for about five years, I don't even see her, and you're saying I'm still not over her?"

"Yes," Marie had stood up, "that's exactly what I'm saying, it's what I see right now, look at yourself, you can't even talk about her calmly."

The blood drained from my temples, I've rarely felt that, in my life. But I tried to stay.

"Never talk to me like that again," I said.

She must have sensed that she'd said too much all at once, and she wanted me to stay, I'm sorry. You have nothing to apologize for, and since I couldn't sleep, after a while I left and caught a taxi. She didn't try to stop me. There were still a lot of people on the square, people around the movie theater, customers from the Brasserie Wepler, and opposite, a long line of people on the sidewalk waiting to buy cigarettes from the little tobacco shop. I waited at the taxi stand until I'd calmed down. It was one o'clock in the morning, maybe that was why. I called Marie. She wasn't completely asleep yet.

"I was hoping you'd call me, are you angry with me?"

"No, I'm fine."

Marie said nothing.

"It's good that you didn't sulk for long."

...

It had been strange, that meal at his place. His place? On the other side of the avenue in La Garenne-Colombes, there were still big glass buildings for banks and insurance companies, with lots of square feet of unused office space, but it would come, with time. On his side of the street, that last block of old houses and apartments where he lived, it had been almost fifty years, shit, I told myself, half a century, since you'd started seeing high-rises going up, and it wasn't finished yet. It would probably never be finished. When I lived in Gennevilliers with Benjamin's mother, I'd watched an apartment building being demolished, the weather was glorious that day. I've never forgotten it. We'd all watched open-mouthed under the blue sky: how had we been able to live where there was nothing left to remind you? The building where I spent my childhood has been repainted several times, it's been years since I last went back there. In his apartment, he had only the basics, a sofa bed, two stools in the kitchen, plus a TV set, there was always at least a TV set everywhere you went. I told Marie about it, how this guy who'd been a good friend had invited us over for dinner. We must have been his first guests in a long time. And in spite of all these differences, he was still in some way a guy like me, there was so much in our lives that came down to chance. Marie was following my lips, maybe she was finding it hard to take an interest in my ramblings, but I kept on all the same.

"Marie, is everything OK?"

We'd gone back to Brochant for a last drink after hav-

ing dinner near my apartment, close by the town hall. She
had some news. She hadn't told me before, but she'd had
to have some tests, actually she was hoping it was a false
alarm. She hadn't wanted to worry me about it. But she
was going to have to go to the hospital for two or three
days. Really? There, now you know everything. Then she
didn't say anything more about it.

There was quite a lot of noise in the café, we looked at
each other, I had nothing more to say either. She was very
patient with me. I felt I wanted to put my arms around
her and hold her tight, in that café in Brochant. I wouldn't
let this one go. Why? How to know? She stopped smiling out into the night when I asked her which hospital?
Beaujon, she said, but the aftercare, if necessary, could be
in a private clinic in Boulogne, she had contacts there. It
would probably be several months. She'd cared for people
all her life, it was strange to her that it was her turn now
to be sick, she'd almost never thought about it before.
And besides, it was too early to know.

"I'll go with you if you want."

She said, would you really? She told me I wasn't
obliged. Then she held out her hand and said to me come,
quickly, let's go back home. We left the bar in Brochant.
She looked out of place among the people in Place Clichy
that night, there were transvestites at the counter, laughing loudly and getting loaded before starting work. She
liked this place a lot. The guys knew her, they would stop
on the boulevard to kiss her, she liked the nightlife. She
would show it to me, she'd already told me about it. As
soon as we closed the door, we kissed, and I told myself
we were doing something important, something precious
and important, I mustn't pull down the curtain, I must
give her all my strength, then it would be all right and we
could do it. I didn't know what it was we could do. But we
could do it. That was what I'd decided. I think that was

the night I started smoking again.

She laughed when I went to get a cigarette and asked me why it was that people smoked after making love. It was a long time since I'd last done that. Yes, absolutely, like a guy younger than me. She drew the sheet over her, all I could see now was that dark hair. By the way, she pointed to a little package on her chest of drawers, against the wall, I have something for you, it's a gift. It was another book by F. Scott Fitzgerald, I hadn't even opened a newspaper since I'd finished the story of the guy who always wants to pull down the curtain.

"Thanks, Marie."

"Are you sleeping here?"

I put the book down. I lay down next to her. She had an appointment the following week, on Tuesday. It wasn't the first time, she'd already had to go in two years ago, and like all normal people she really hated it. And yet she'd done it all her life. She was scared of hearing really bad news this time, she wasn't sure what to think. I realized there were birds talking to us, down below, on the boulevard near the Brochant metro station. Was it really the 17th arrondissement here? During our separation my wife had lived in Wagram, a big studio apartment lent to her by a girlfriend, but Wagram and Brochant were nothing like each other. Marie got to sleep very late. Soon after that, since I couldn't sleep, I went into the kitchen with the book she'd given me. I felt good like that. We all go in the same direction, often, when it's night. Tomorrow, I'd have to go back to work and hide my tiredness in order not to look like a worn-out old guy who's lost interest in everything. I'd call guys on the phone and sound worried, I'd talk about things I really knew nothing about, pretty much like everyone else, and then, in the employee cafeteria or at a restaurant with colleagues, I'd be brought up to date on the news of the day. How about you, what's new? Well, as you can see, the curtain hasn't quite been pulled down yet. Marie has cancer. Nothing new apart from that. How about you? Er, me? Well, just like you. Yeah, the same. Above all, there'd be the new regulations, stories about the office, new arrivals and imminent departures, and then, after a pointless day, I'd probably be very tired. Where had I read that story about a young boy born tired, who couldn't stand his tiredness, as if it was growing along with him, or something like that? Marie tossed and turned in her bad dreams. After that, I had the impression she was fast asleep.

Below Place de Clichy, there were two hours of complete peace and quiet about four in the morning. All the same, you can sense that the city isn't completely asleep. The day gives Place de Clichy a hangover, one that only night can get rid of. Is that why it breathes softly, like the living dead? Benjamin had decided on the date of his departure, at the end of May. That upset him a little too, but anyway. I walked out of the bedroom again and waited for morning, looking through the window for the signs the shadows were giving me, the shadows of the leaves on the trees and of the lone guys with their stooped shoulders, I know them well, those lone guys with their stooped shoulders. I was going to have a lot of things to do in the next few weeks. That scared me a little because I wasn't used to it. I often thought about that when I saw how Marc-André lived, he had an important job, children from two marriages, and still found time to be there for me, and for others too. He'd always been there. At a certain point, Marie murmured something. I tiptoed back inside to see her. Her eyes were open, just above the sheet and the blankets. She closed them again when she saw me. Afterwards, we waited for morning, all the things that were in store for us, even if we didn't want them. The birds in the acacias on the corner of the street were already ready, because the night was coming to an end.

"Do you think it'll be all right?"

"Of course," I said, "Of course it'll be all right. I'll go with you to Beaujon if you want."

That morning, she didn't put on her make-up right away, like she had before. I liked her confidence. I often get attached to stupid things, because, without those things, nothing could really bring us together. But I see that only now, after all those failures and all those years.

"It doesn't hurt, it's strange. It doesn't hurt at all."

I lit a cigarette, now that I was going to start smoking again for real, outside my office building, at home, on the scooter, and the thing I really rediscovered that morning was my good old cough, it had never quite left me. We'd have to wait for the results of the other tests anyway. Do you think so? I already knew Beaujon Hospital. I'd been there myself a few years ago, and before that too. I didn't tell Marie, obviously. When I left, she asked me to hold her tight, there was nothing else she could do now, we'd talked for a long time. All those wasted months faded away. I went back to work. There would always be work for a guy like me. Besides, we had a whole bunch of things to do, a lot of young guys had started in the last few months, with degrees in things that didn't exist before. I was nicknamed the old man, which didn't really say much. Their stories, their love affairs too, their all-too-obvious ambitions, their meals in the cafeteria where I no longer set foot, their passion for computers and worthless movies, it really was a new world. Benjamin was my only link with them. Sometimes it made me smile, we'd helped each other out for years on end. Well, anyway.

I took advantage of the lunch break to call Marie, she hadn't done much. She'd gone for a walk along the end of the boulevard, around Porte de Clichy, and then the Cité des Fleurs, do you know it? Yes, I know it well. She'd sat there for a while. She hadn't wanted to leave.

"I'm scared you'll dump me."

I didn't answer. I thought no, why would I dump you? I'll never dump you, Marie. Then we chatted for a while, I should have called her from a phone booth, I told myself, seeing colleagues pass, it embarrassed me. We'd talk again that evening. When she hung up, I think she was pleased. She would never tell me, I already knew that about her, but if I sensed it, she wouldn't bother to hide it from me. Marie had nothing to hide, to tell the truth. And then I waited for evening. I left the office a little while after the others. I was pleased to be going home. I'd spent so many years completely alone, they were part of me now, and even the presence of a woman might weigh on me from time to time. Was I too old already? In the years after my divorce, I'd been in a cold rage that made me talk to myself for hours on end. Guys at the office would look at me strangely sometimes. But I didn't notice, and besides, most of the time I couldn't help it. I often think of those wasted years of anger, where did they get me?

It was Marco who'd said: listen, you have to do something, I'm sorry to have to tell you, but you're going a little bit crazy, you can't carry on like this.

"You're not going to start, too?"

We talked a lot, for whole evenings, he and I. Then some time later, we had to reverse roles, his son had been arrested several times for some drug-related thing, and Marc-André couldn't carry on burying his head in the sand, Antoine had been sentenced to six months. He would take him to rehab when he got out of prison. Antoine had been shooting up for a long time. During that period, I'd slept with a whole bunch of women, it hadn't lasted long, almost all of them had suggested a plan of action, that's what they all said, a plan of action, but he was the only one I accepted those words from. How many of them there were, guys like me! The shrink I saw looked like he didn't sleep well at night. Was it because he made me come to his office at seven in the morning? I skipped several sessions, sometimes for legitimate reasons, but he didn't care at all. He looked grumpily at the checks, he preferred to be paid in cash; he was a strange man. Why was I thinking about that now? I was a bit scared for Marie, but also, beneath that, I was scared for no reason, just plain fear, there was always a good reason to be scared, most of the time.

4

THERE HE WAS, IN FRONT OF ME, SITTING ON THE STAIRS.
He was looking at his shoes, and I didn't know if he was
really looking at them or if he was doing it to hide his embarrassment, a bit like a big child. He was the last thing
I needed in my life right now, he was only a side issue.
But I smiled at him all the same, and we shook hands. He
didn't need to move, because of the height of the steps,
when he looked up I knew what it was that struck me so
much about his appearance: he had all his hair, and it was
very brown, with hardly a single white hair. I remembered
his mother, suddenly.

"I'm not disturbing you, am I?" he asked in a flat voice.
"I was in the neighborhood."

"Oh, really?" I replied good-humoredly. In his situation, I think I'd have thought up a better excuse. But I
can't really be sure of anything. He stood up, I asked him
to excuse me while I looked in my mailbox. In the past
few years, looking in my mailbox has stopped making me
anxious, I'm not paying alimony to Benjamin's mother
anymore. For a long time, I only had to be a few days
late to find the bailiff's papers in the mailbox. Now I'm
more scared of news you don't expect, news about people
from the old days; we knew them and loved them, or we
didn't know them well and didn't like them much, but
they catch up with us and tell us they're dead, or sick, or
alive and well and looking for traces of their past. Any-

way, there was nothing in the mailbox that day.

"How are you fixed for time? Come up and have a drink."

"I don't want to disturb you," he repeated, and at that point, the desire to make fun of him came over me again, we waited for the elevator.

He looked through the window, then, from the buildings in the distance, he shifted his gaze to the end of my street, which was even livelier in April. I'd put down my briefcase and taken off my jacket, he turned toward me. For a brief moment, we looked at each other without saying anything. I think my mind was elsewhere. On the way home I'd had the idea of suggesting to Benjamin that he come for dinner one of these evenings. He was very busy with his preparations for leaving, and the closer it got, the less they felt like living in Zurich. Who wanted to be twenty-seven in a place like that, in the research lab of a big chemical company? That's why I think Jean's visit must have felt like an intrusion. Why had he chosen me, me rather than Marc-André, who'd actually found him a job? Was it because I live alone, and he doesn't?

"Don't just stand there, sit down. What's going on?"

He resumed the same vague air, as if worried by the drafty air, just like earlier on the stairs.

"I don't know. I won't stay long."

I made up my mind not to let myself be irritated by his remarks. During all those years of being unemployed and on welfare, he'd always been idle, and maybe that kind of dialogue was the only kind he could bring off.

"Is it the job?"

He gave me a weary, slightly boyish smile. "Yes, they're real oddballs, things haven't gotten better with the years, from what I can see ... Didn't Marc-André say anything?"

His tone just a little shrill, falsely mild, no, I don't know anything. He was the same age as us and he talked like a teenager, and not just any teenager. I handed him a beer, and he took the top off it as if he was scared that if he did it badly he might blow up the building.

"Do you want a glass?"

"No, thanks." He stood up. "I'd like to talk to you. Tell me if you have something to do, you're not obligated to listen to me."

All the same, he'd chosen me, he explained why me as he went along. We talked what, two or three hours, something like that? I confess I'd forgotten a lot of things from the old days, and even from the last few years of my life, but I remembered them completely thanks to him. Sometimes his voice was hoarse, sometimes it was only a thin thread. It began at school according to him, when he'd been moved to technical high school. Do you remember? Yes, I remembered. He'd spent a year in that school at Quatre-Routes, he'd been separated from us, Marco and me and the others, that was where he'd first been affected. He was speaking slowly too. That surprised me, because to be honest I'd have expected more vehemence on his part. He'd had a bad patch that lasted several months, he'd stayed in bed in his room, his mother was the concierge of an apartment building. Yes, I remembered.

I think I can even see him in those days. I remember the big covered entrance next to the little record store on the square by the station where we used to buy 45s. I remember a woman with very white skin, and the black hair that she wore pulled back. He was fifteen, and he couldn't get out of bed. He'd lost the will to live. But that didn't mean he wanted to die, and although he couldn't explain it, all his life it had affected him from time to time. He'd finished his beer. I offered him another. I told myself that we were going to spend all night like this, if only I could find a way to cut things short, then, afterwards, I stopped thinking about it. He'd recovered without knowing why, that first time. He'd been to see several doctors in Paris, his mother had made inquiries. She was intelligent and very poor. He still loved her as much as ever. The doctors talked to them about adolescence, severe depression, attacks of melancholia. He told me that, attacks of melancholia, with a slightly self-satisfied smile. Melancholia. Not without hope, it seems to me, he repeated the word several times, as if it might make him more interesting. After a while, I realized he was talking almost in the dark, and I suggested we go into the kitchen, maybe he'd like to stay and have a bite to eat? I locked myself in the bathroom for five minutes and phoned Marie to tell her I had an unexpected visitor. I'd call her back later, how late would be OK? He'd taken up his favorite position, on a stool. He kept his arms crossed. When I asked him to take a stick of butter from the refrigerator, he noticed the drawings by Benjamin that I'd kept, some of them were almost fifteen years old. There'd been a time when my son always made a drawing for me when he left on Sunday night. It seems to me these drawings protect us, him and me, even though, in a way, it'd be better if I removed them. Under magnets, I also keep urgent notes, reminders of things to do, and tickets from the dry cleaner. He smiled as he looked at them, as if he didn't quite believe them. That's your son, Benjamin, isn't it? How old is he now?

He continued his life story in broad strokes, but, as always, he kept coming back to his childhood, his life with his mother, it was just the two of them. Then he told me about his first love, a girl he'd met at the skating rink in Asnières. Do you know it? Yes, I knew it. A vague smile came and died on his lips, once again, when I confirmed that yes, I knew it, I knew where it was, or I vaguely remembered some figure from Asnières or Colombes, La Garenne, all those places of ours from the old days. We'd been there together, in the old days. He hadn't heard from this woman in three or four years. In all that time he'd had more or less nothing but welfare to live on. His mother also helped him a little, as best she could, since he had told her his situation. He'd hung around. He'd stripped wallpaper, kicked his heels outside DIY centers hoping to be hired for the day. He'd learned the geography of night shelters, municipal baths, and food banks. It wasn't really new to him, his mother and he had always lived hand to mouth. I thought again about the ground-floor apartment he'd invited us to. The open window onto the inner courtyard. Those windows would have to be repainted almost every year. The family opposite, a couple and their two children, I remembered the little girl sitting on her tricycle, the clumsily paved-over cobblestones. He'd loved that girl. As only guys like me can, he said, and I filed his expression away in a corner of my mind to try to understand it. And what about me? I realized that he chose these high-flown phrases because he found it hard to explain things more deeply. I didn't dare interrupt him, he didn't stop talking while we ate.

Ben called me around nine, he wanted to know if I could help with the move. He was going to put some things in a storage facility, you know, the one at the industrial dock in Gennevilliers?

"Yes, listen, I have a friend here. I'll call you on Tuesday, OK?"

Jean was watching me, waiting for me to finish so that he could continue. So, what happened to that girl? He smiled, rather like the way an adult would smile at someone who doesn't understand because he lacks experience.

"Her name is Adeline Vlasquez, do you know her?"

I made an effort to remember, not so much at the time, but occasionally in the days that followed, even sometimes at work when I thought about his story or let myself go and escaped into the past. Did she also go to Le Cercle, the bistro in Asnières? He nodded, yes. They were in love, at least he'd known that in his life, he was already twenty-four when they met. At that time he was working at the FNAC, the megastore, he was one of their first employees, in the days when it still meant something to work at FNAC. He made me laugh without meaning to. They'd set up house together, they were lucky and even found a little house on the hill at Puteaux at the beginning of the '80s, before the property boom. They'd made plans for the future, and then, without warning, that fatigue of his had struck again. He'd had to quit his job. She thought he was doing drugs, or that he was cheating on her, she thought a whole bunch of things, and in spite of his efforts she ended up becoming tired of him, she'd left him two years after the election of François Mitterrand. By the time he was done, we'd finished dinner. He'd been talking for nearly two hours.

"You must be fed up, I'm boring you with my stories."

"Why do you say that?"

He'd been telling me the life story of a guy like me, when it came down to it, but one where every episode took place between attacks of what he called his fatigue. For several years now, since Germany, where he'd earned a good living in a factory making machine tools, he'd been scraping up money from wherever he could, he loved welfare. Without it, he'd probably be dead. He'd lived a totally useless life (big smile). Later, talking with Marco, I realized that he was inexhaustible on the subject, how to live on nothing, how to make do with only the basics for as long as possible.

I suggested we move to the living room. I made coffee and he waited, his eyes turned toward the lights in the odd-numbered houses, as if he was at the movies, a spectator of his own life. We all are, obviously. No, he'd never seriously tried to live with a woman again, he'd never forgotten Adeline Vlasquez. All the same, he'd waited several years before he tried to track her down. His eyes shone as they looked at the suburb outside, for no reason, just uttering her name. He had done it, one day. It was just before meeting us again, Marco and me. I was starting to wonder what he wanted from me, apart from talking. It hadn't been easy to find her. She'd kept the same name. She didn't want to believe him, after all these years that hadn't changed her one bit. She'd lived in England, after their separation she'd let herself be led on by guys for a while. Then, and he gave me his weary smile, too big and also too slow, she'd come back. She'd always had work, apparently. He told me that in a pensive tone. She was one of those women who search desperately for a man to have children with, but sometimes that takes their whole lives. Are you still angry? I asked him. He said yes, she asked me to stop harassing her. Harassing, he repeated slowly. Can you imagine? It was after midnight.

Now I wanted to get rid of him, I'd had enough of people like that around me in my life, I'd also had enough of my own memories. And yet, I don't really know what it was, something stopped me from dismissing him with the excuse that I had work tomorrow, or that I'd already spent all that time listening to him talking, about his failed life, about everything and nothing. Adeline Vlasquez. It's lasted my whole life, he murmured. He was smoking hand-rolled cigarettes with blue Samson tobacco, like when we were all together, during our years in high school.

"Will you roll me one, please?"

I held his hand as he lit my cigarette. His eyes were sad, seen from close-up. I decided I'd do what I could for him, if I could.

"And how's it going now with your job?"

He smiled again in his clownish way, his face still as weary. "You must be joking, I haven't been out in a week."

I really think he wanted to laugh.

"You're the first person I've seen in all that time."

He stopped speaking. He often had these pauses, long ones, as if he'd gone somewhere and gotten lost on the way back, and nobody knew the name of the place. I realized it was Adeline Vlasquez country. It was a long way away, somewhere in the past, but he'd never been able to tell the difference between then and now. I think I remembered that we were good friends in the old days, but he'd never forgotten.

In the days that followed I often thought about that, and even when I told Marco about it, I wasn't able to put a face to the name, even though I flatter myself that I never forget a face. Maybe it isn't true, then? He'd untied his shoelaces, he was sitting there stiffly, leaning back in the armchair. I bought two of them on a whim when I first moved into this apartment, I must have been forty-six, something like that. I bought them six months later, they looked exactly like the ones my mother had bought when I was fourteen. I never sat down facing her, in one of the two armchairs. In my place she would put linen that needed darning, shirts I'd lost buttons from, and more often still, papers to be sorted. My mother had a genius for sorting, and it really drove her crazy during my childhood years. It was as if she spent my childhood sorting it into files. It struck me it would be too late to call Marie. Sometimes, our lives accelerated, and then it took us years to stem the overflow. She would understand anyway. Would she sleep tonight, or else, like the last night we'd spent together, the previous week, would she wait for me to sleep and then get up and stand by the window in her kitchen for a long time, all by herself, without switching the light on? After a while, he seemed to realize that I was there, and he looked at his watch, conspicuously, like someone who wants you to know he's looking at his watch.

"Wow, I have to get going. Is it really two o'clock?"

I shrugged. I didn't feel like driving him home.

"You can sleep here if you like, I don't mind."

He looked at me, his smile was ironic. It irritated me a little but it really was late, and I had a lot of things to do the next day.

"I get up early, all you have to do is pull the door shut behind you."

By the time I left the bathroom, he'd rolled himself up in the blanket I'd given him, and the clearest image I still have of him from that evening, when he'd told me his whole life story, is the one of his big hand on the blanket when he said good night. And the name of that woman he'd loved badly all his life, Adeline Vlasquez. Goodnight. Yes, you too. I'll call you. OK. I thought about F. Scott Fitzgerald. All life is a process of breaking down, where had he said that? I set my alarm for seven. At night I don't have much time to look at my face and the damage it wears, or even the first brown age spots already appearing on my hands. Was he just skipping work, or had he called in sick? I hadn't asked him. I'd find out soon enough anyway. He didn't really seem to care. In any case, I wasn't short of work. You just had to be there, not let anything show, six more years of this pace and I'd be out of it.

. . .

I had some strange dreams that night. We were teenagers, Marco and I and our girlfriends, and we were doing séances, I'd always enjoyed that. I saw myself doing it. I fell asleep at Le Cercle, I think it was. I didn't see Adeline Vlasquez there. Then there were dreams that didn't make any sense at all, with big fish and funerals and things. I thought I saw him walking in his underpants along the hallway where my bedroom is, I never close my bedroom door. Later, I also saw a woman, probably Marie, creeping about in a park, was it the park of the organization near Beaujon? She must have been about a hundred and was carrying a big bloodstained knife in her hand and singing a love song, *India Song*. That woke me before seven. I'd seen that movie a very long time ago. Benjamin and I loved the song from it. I got up without making a noise, and when I switched on the light in the kitchen, I saw the blanket neatly folded on the sofa bed, he'd already left. I don't know what made me go to the window and look out. There he was, on the sidewalk opposite, sitting on the bench by the bus stop for routes 115, 341, and 207 A and B. I didn't need to imagine him in a dream, he really was a guy like me. It was weird, the way he'd come back into my life, as quickly as he was going to leave it now, but for how much longer?

I let the curtain fall gently. Why was he still sitting there? Was he waiting for a sign from me, like a runaway child or indeed a guy who was lost? I don't know. Neither did Marc-André when I called him from the office during the lunch break and told him about our evening. I hadn't been able to wipe out the image I had of him, early in the morning, sitting at the bus stop. Which one had he taken? The A went right through the middle of La Garenne-Colombes, I remember. Now he was nothing more than a guy filled with regrets, incapable of holding down a job. Especially as, and Marco knew this, he had a nasty temper. Does he really? I heard him laughing at the other end, gravely. You could say that. I know what I'm talking about. He'd called him to keep him abreast of his problems with his employer. He hadn't been too sure what to do, although he'd often had the desire to just hang up the phone, and that would have been the end of it.

"You never did it?"

"No, I thought things were getting better."

Then we talked about something else. Did he remember a girl called Adeline Vlasquez? He thought about it, but no, he couldn't remember. It didn't mean much to Marco and me. Our memory wavers, it has no middle, like fishing lines on the cloudy surface of the water. Marco told me he had to go, unfortunately. Aïcha wanted to know when she could meet Marie. How does she know? I asked Marco.

"I must have mentioned her without meaning to. All right, then, bye, I really must go."

In a sense it's always good, when we hang up on each other, because we could spend our whole lives making small talk about this and that, but I may be imagining things. We're always more alone than we suppose, I think.

...

I also think I was relieved, in the end, to see him leave my apartment. I'd invited him in, we'd done our best to help him get back on his feet, and now he really had to walk by himself. I don't like thinking these things, saying these words. They made me think of the father I didn't have. I never talked like that to Benjamin, or I would have had the impression I was someone else. I didn't say anything to Benjamin, to tell the truth. I regret it sometimes, obviously. There was a time when I often went for a walk during my lunch break over to his elementary school, then later to his high school, when the classes were coming out, on Fridays when I could wait for him. I'd keep myself at a distance so as not to embarrass him. I didn't intend it that way, but I was using him to give meaning to my life, after our separation. I'd forgotten exactly why we'd separated. I'd had affairs, and probably so had she, but I think more than anything that there were other things she wanted to do with her life, and she didn't think she could do them with me. I'd disappointed her too. I'd always hoped, I think. She suddenly came out with the idea of a divorce one Sunday evening, that afternoon we'd gone for a walk with Benjamin in the Buttes-Chaumont. We'd eaten ice cream on the square outside the town hall of the 19th arrondissement. I remember the flavors he chose, chocolate and lemon. After that, we weren't able to speak anymore. She'd already found a lawyer, she'd been planning it all for a long time, everything was worked out in her head. It took me several months to realize. What had I done to get to that point, were they all like me? It had taken Marco less than three months to decide to live together with Aïcha. All the same, my son and I had never stopped loving each other. He never blamed me.

"Why did you and Mom end it?"

He asked me that once, a few years ago. He hadn't met Anaïs yet, but had been dumped by the girl who'd been the love of his life from tenth grade to senior year, they'd just broken up. I liked the girl a lot too, the three of us had been on vacation together two years running, once to Brittany, and another time to the Baie de Somme, Marco had let us use a house he'd bought there. He was desperate, my son, and all the words I could have said, looking at his distraught face, I kept to myself.

"I'm not sure anymore, Ben. It happened gradually with your mother and me, we loved each other a lot."

"Is that true?"

That time, his eyes had lit up, and then we quickly left the café where we were because he'd started crying again. He was heartbroken. He'd never see her again. He didn't think he could live without her. He didn't know what to do. And then in the end, obviously, he did know. He was twenty-one when they broke up. Do you mind if I pull down the curtain? It was a nice story, but it wasn't always enough to pull it down. Sometimes, you had to go even deeper.

5

ON THE DAYS THAT FOLLOWED, THERE WAS A LOT OF RAIN.
The Seine was very high. I could spend hours watching it
when it's like that. I often went to Brochant, Marie was
fairly well, I thought. We both knew what she was waiting
for. It was always there between us. But we almost never
talked about it. Sometimes, she'd drift off for an hour
or two, sitting on her couch without moving, and it was
good to be there next to her at moments like that. I took
some extra days off that I was owed from the previous
year, I really needed them. I was glad I could do that. I
could live without my job for a week and concentrate on
myself. The girl looked at the computer screen and even
said: at last! I went to a whole lot of places, I did a lot of
things, the kind of things you're always putting off until
later and end up never doing. Most of the time it's as if
these things are only there to make us think about them
without ever going anywhere near them. I went to see
Benjamin when he left his lab in Jussieu, we walked for
a while along the Seine, it was brown or gray, and quite
swollen. We were near the Gare d'Austerlitz, it seemed
odd to me to be in a part of Paris where I almost never
set foot when I'm not working. We walked for a long time
without saying anything, after we'd talked about work, his
move, his new job in Zurich, Anaïs, what did she think
about it? She wasn't exactly delighted, but it'd be OK.
They'd see, anyway. He'd reached a dead end here. There

was only Switzerland or the United States left. That made me smile, I think. I'd have been incapable of studying the things he did. Was his mother gifted for that kind of thing? I couldn't remember. We had a drink at the counter of an Auvergnese café in the Gare d'Austerlitz. We played the lottery cards. Ben won one euro fifty. We had another beer, and then lost three times. We then crossed the Seine and walked to the Gare de Lyon, to take Line 14 on the metro.

That was where we had to say goodbye, I'd continue on to visit Marie, and he would go home by train. And then I changed my mind. I told him about her on the platform at the Gare Saint-Lazare. It was the right moment, I thought. For a long time, whenever I waited for him on Friday, at the end of the platform, I used to see lots of guys on their own also waiting to see their kids for the weekend. We didn't speak to each other, but we recognized each other in the end. The people on the opposite platform were just getting off the train when I told my son I was seeing somebody, her name was Marie. I don't know if I said it loudly enough or not, he said who? Marie? He read my lips and he just smiled, oh really, has it been long? No, we chatted for quite a long time, but we've really only been seeing each other for a month ... I felt a bit stupid, saying all that. Will you get married again? My son had often asked me that when he was in his late teens. His mother didn't have any more children. She lived for a few years with a guy from Asnières, a dentist, also divorced. I don't know why it didn't work out. I'd have had other children, I think, if I'd forgotten more easily. Forgiven too. In these past few years, I'd had nothing but brief encounters. A woman on a street corner, with her indifferent smile and eyes. It happened like that, and it's nothing. An evening, a year. With Sylvie, almost two years. You don't have many real encounters in a lifetime.

Night bars, flashing your debit card, and aspirin the next morning. Another guy's wife, the lies that are true when you tell them, and then you forget you told them. People are well-behaved on the train. Those who aren't using their cell phones all the time look out the windows, not many people talk apart from that. Ben sat down on a fold-up seat, his legs slightly parted. He hadn't said anything at all about Marie. Maybe because it had taken me all that time to consider living with another woman? Otherwise, I don't know. Maybe I was imagining things, because he'd be going soon and I'd be on my own, even though I didn't see him very much anyway. He gave a little sign with his hand, then he took his MP3 from the pocket of his bag and for a guy like me, a father every other weekend and for half of every vacation, that has to last two weeks, for years on end.

My heart was pounding. I became aware of it on the steps at Cour de Rome, after the escalator. I went and killed time at the FNAC in Saint-Lazare, waiting for seven o'clock, Marie wouldn't be back before eight, there was no point in hurrying. I looked at the books by F. Scott Fitzgerald, I'd already read two of them. I didn't know which of the others to choose, and I didn't want to ask the assistants. At the snack bar on the second floor, people take what they've just bought out of their bags, or else they're waiting for something. I used to come here often a few years ago, to the FNAC in Saint-Lazare. It isn't an especially pleasant place, it's just there with the idea that, between purchases, people should take the trouble to talk to each other, because after all they live together, for better or worse. I don't remember why I went there so often, on the weekends when I didn't have Benjamin. I've spent a lot of time in that area since my teenage years. I used to wait for my son at the Gare Saint-Lazare, on Saturdays. Once, I'd spotted him and his mother on Rue de Caumartin, it was a sunny day, he must have been telling her one of those endless stories that came into his head sometimes, and he looked perfectly happy, without me. I remember I smiled like an idiot in their direction, and then, when I realized, I went and took refuge in the snack bar on the second floor of FNAC. There, women wait for their girlfriends so that they can go to the movies, notch up another one on their schedule, or, where guys like me are concerned, they drink coffee and wait for it to pass, and end up deciding not to approach their children when they see them on the street, on the sidewalk of Caumartin. It felt strange to me to be on vacation at this time of the year. I'm one of those guys for whom work has become a kind of blessing, it stops you from having to think, basically. Several times in the past few years, I've tried to calculate the number of hours I've spent in offices, receiving people, making phone calls, or reading files without the slightest interest, I've never been very good at counting. I didn't always think about Marie, far from it, but the nearer the time came for her to go into the hospital, the more I thought about things I'd like to do with her if she wanted. Sometimes, at night, I had obvious nightmares about her illness, and I was afraid she'd read them on my face when she woke up. In the end, I didn't buy anything, I got up and left.

I walked toward La Trinité, it was one of the places in Paris where I'd spent most time in my life, as a teenager, when I hung out with Marco, and later, during my divorce and my two years of unemployment. But without my realizing it, almost nothing from those days is still there. A few years ago, they even replaced the red Coca-Cola sign on the building at the end of Rue d'Amsterdam with a green Perrier sign. Am I the only person who's interested in that kind of detail? Passage du Havre, with its salesgirls and its prostitutes, has disappeared. It's been replaced by chains and franchises. You get straight to the metro through the shopping mall. On Rue Saint-Lazare, there's still that coffee merchant's, Méo, I used to be taken there when I was a boy, to buy good coffee. When I approached the store, I realized I was quite moved and didn't want to go home. Smells don't change. I hadn't gotten over it. I mustn't let Marie see me like this. It never lasts a long time, with me. I almost lingered in the Square de la Trinité but it was closed. The local homeless had settled on the steps of the church. I would never have burned a candle in that one, I realized that. I walked around the outside of the little park and then up Rue de Clichy, which is very gray and is really one of those streets in Paris where to be honest nothing happens except that time passes, nobody ever goes there except people on their own, with bags and newspapers and umbrellas. I'd told Benjamin again that I wanted a scooter, and he'd laughed. But I think he'd understood. If I didn't want to pull down the curtain too soon, it was becoming urgent that I get out a bit more. I felt a bit drawn to number 23 on that street. That was where my ex-wife and I had spent our first night together, in the apartment of a friend of hers. I still remembered it very well, from time to time. I turned around. I searched for her name in my head without finding it. I had to be careful, I didn't want to start rambling out loud, with a name on the tip of my tongue, and worn-out old images that were of no concern to anyone but me. I quickly got to Brochant.

Marie was waiting for me so that we could go out. She wasn't too tired. She'd made herself look beautiful tonight. She'd put on all her bracelets. She simply wanted to walk along the boulevard one more time, do you mind? I took her hand, of course I didn't mind. She'd had a phone call from the department where she was going to be operated on. They were expecting her tomorrow, in the afternoon. Now that she had told me the news, she simply wanted to walk as far as Place de Clichy, where we were already kind of regulars at the Brasserie Wepler, a secret just for us. People had their favorite tables, and it was always a kind of victory—but over what, death? The chestnut trees on the boulevard were in full blossom now. She smiled whenever she turned to look at me, but when she looked away, I saw only a beautiful woman with her arm through mine, with hundreds of things in her head she didn't feel the need to tell me, not me, not anybody. There were lots of people on the boulevard, because of the fine weather. At one point she stopped to talk to a guy, he'd recently been taken care of by her organization, he was all pretty and sparkling, if you can say that. In his fancy dress, he'd be starting work in a few hours, he blew a kiss at her. Marie smiled at him. Yes, see you soon! The chestnut trees smelled almost too strong on the streets around the square. When we'd had enough of walking, we went to the Brasserie Wepler, she squeezed my hand with her fingertips.

"Are you all right, Marie, what are you thinking about?"

She looked at me and her smile froze, even though she'd been making a big effort to put a brave face on it.

"I've really liked it here, all these people. I've really liked my life here."

I kissed her to shut her up. I told her to stop talking nonsense like that, especially on Place de Clichy, in the brasserie where she'd been a regular as a single woman, and then I told her that with her I was getting back into the idea of living as a couple, being together, for better or, in this particular case, from tomorrow anyway, for worse or something like it.

We were lucky: we found a good table. She asked me to tell her about my life that evening.

"My life?"

I told her that Benjamin was leaving soon. She looked at me closely, I don't know what expression I had on my face, telling her that. It soon got dark, we chatted for a long time. Did I have photographs? I had several of him, but for a few years now there had been fewer opportunities. Marie told me she would really like to meet him, I said he'd like to meet her too, and I'd like it too, I really would. I don't have photos of myself as a child. Marie only asked me the right questions that evening, I think. Afterwards we tried to make plans for the future in the Brasserie Wepler. We were near the ATM in the corner, and with each person that withdrew money, we wanted to ask how they'd been doing in their life, day by day, all this time?

"He has your smile, he does take after you."

"Benjamin?"

"Yes."

I took her hand, and without saying anything, I made a personal vow, the kind that only guys like me make, not to dump her during the treatment or when she came out of Beaujon. The evening before, we'd had a few drinks with Marco and Aïcha. They'd gotten along well, Marc-André had made us laugh, everything was fine. In passing, he told me about Jean. He'd simply quit his job without warning. Thanks to Langinieux, they'd waited a while to see if he'd come back, but by now he'd almost certainly been fired. He wouldn't get any severance payment, obviously. Since then nobody had heard from him. Then Marie and I also talked a little about Marco and Aïcha, I liked telling the story, how he had met her at the clinic at work, how he'd realized a whole lot of things all at the same time, and hadn't looked back since, and neither had she. There we were, the two of us, in the noise of Place de Clichy. Marie didn't want to leave. To talk, to keep talking, until tomorrow. Do you mind if I pull down the curtain?

"Would you like something else, Marie?"

"Yes, how about champagne, what do you think?"

We celebrated that night. And also tomorrow. No, later than tomorrow. Not too late in any case. We had already drunk several times together, she liked drinking, and besides, nobody would celebrate for us if we didn't, so we might as well get on with it ourselves. Marie likes living at night. I understood now the strange hours she kept when we'd met on the dating website. After a while, she stopped talking and lit a cigarette, the guy brought us our glasses. He looked a little like Jean. Lots of people were coming out of the Pathé multiplex, we watched them walking away. I don't like that theater very much. I'm used to small movie houses, the ones you enter and leave furtively, because you go there on your own, that was in the old days, you don't want to disturb the images you keep to yourself, they keep us warm for a while before they're forgotten.

"What are we drinking to? Shall we drink to us?"

To you, to us, to our ... We didn't say anything more. She finished her glass, it wasn't very good quality champagne, but never mind, we were fine that evening. Fewer people on the streets. And then the first guys like me.

"Shall we go, Marie ?

We set off on foot, slowly, to the Brochant metro station, right on the corner, a very attractive, heavily made-up brown-haired guy stopped next to her and gave her a big kiss, then hugged me before disappearing into the night, toward La Condamine. He didn't seem drunk, though. Do you know him? Yes, Marie smiled, he's a patient, look! He's better now.

...

She'd gotten her bag ready in the hallway, we'd have more time tomorrow. I immediately liked that bag, because we'd promised each other we'd go traveling. It was stupid, obviously. We both sat down together, and now, after never telling me anything about the past, as if she'd wanted to live without it, she took out a photograph album. She'd promised me earlier, in the café. There was her name in red on the edge, she'd had that album for a long time. She smiled as she showed it to me. A couple of times, she skipped quickly over a page, that isn't interesting, I didn't ask her anything, because it seems to me that when you come down to it, I already knew. She'd lived in Spain, Morocco, Mali, and New Caledonia. Several trips to Canada. There you are, now you know everything. What do you mean, I know everything? I'd really like to go to Canada with you. I'd suggested that without thinking, it had come out by itself. Are you serious, do you want to? Yes, of course. We should also go and see Benjamin and Anaïs in Zurich, even though Zurich isn't known for its tourist attractions. We'll see.

We went into the bedroom. I was no longer a guy like me at that exact moment, I think. It was a long time since I'd last made love, with love I mean, it did exist after all. It was both very simple and at the same time, not enough. Marie had held out so far. Around two in the morning, she got up, as she usually did, I pretended to sleep in order not to disturb her. After a moment I got up. She was drinking a glass of water and smoking a cigarette, I went to her and we waited for morning together, in each other's arms on the couch. The shutters weren't closed. She'd never wanted to close the shutters since she'd left home the day she turned eighteen. I can understand that, I don't like closed doors in my apartment. We were like each other in some ways, she had breast cancer but apart from that, the prognosis was uncertain. She'd delayed a little too long, they hadn't found any secondary cancers. There are birds that sing around five-thirty in the morning, at the end of May, in the area of Place de Clichy. I thought about the song by Mano Solo that Benjamin had listened to endlessly, not so long ago, on Place de Clichy, he'd made me a recording of it. It had gotten into my head and I was unable to forget it. Since his childhood he must have made a dozen CDs for me. Over the years, I must have listened to them endlessly, in the car, in the morning, or in the kitchen when I was making something to eat, alone, on weekends. I took a shower, trying not to make any noise. She was asleep now.

I waited a little while longer before going down to find croissants for breakfast. It was very important for me to do that. I couldn't take her fear on myself, I couldn't take her tumor, but I could always go down and look for croissants for breakfast, and in a few hours, we'd both go by car to Beaujon. She'd asked me to pick up her mail. She'd also had money problems for a time, she'd almost lost this apartment, because she'd been negligent about the dates, things that are normal for guys like me, if nothing new happens to them that transports them elsewhere, like a big wave on the ocean. We left around noon. We stopped at the pizzeria in Clichy where I often go with Marco, but Marie couldn't swallow a thing anyway. It's a big hospital, Beaujon. She was walking just a little way behind me, I didn't want to turn around toward her. She'd pushed me in front when we got to the good wing of the building. Yes, she had all her papers ready. She handed them to the woman at the admissions desk, with a smile, as if none of this was about her. Marie was used to hospitals and clinics, people who are sick and also die, sometimes. There were no private rooms.

She insisted and I went to see if I could help, but no, nothing could be done, not for the moment. In hospitals, there aren't many private rooms, and they're reserved for the most serious cases. She'd been hiding her panic well, but now, without my knowing exactly how it had happened, I could feel it rising inside her. It was on her lips, but never spilled over. We finally came to an agreement with the admissions people. She could change rooms as soon as possible. In the meantime, she'd be in 115. She had no idea how long she'd spend there, only a few days at first, but afterwards? The woman in the bed beside hers couldn't have been older than thirty. But most of the others in the ward were distinctly older than Marie. She told me very soon, maybe two weeks after they started the treatment, that she couldn't stand the unfairness of it, suffering the same thing as people much older than her, do you realize, why is it happening to me?

When we got there, her neighbor in the ward was reading *Elle*, she nodded at Marie, that was all. From that floor you could see the wing of the great building added to Beaujon and behind it, toward the Seine, that was where I came from. Ever since I was born, I'd seen that hospital. Along with the Seine, it was part of my first landscape. Marie looked at the empty closet, and when she'd finished her inspection of that emptiness, she said can you leave me please? I said yes, all right. I looked for words I couldn't find, but a woman like Marie doesn't need too many words, especially at moments like these.

She was due to be operated on the day after tomorrow, she'd already seen the anesthesiologist. We said goodbye. She walked me to the door of the ward. I turned around to look at her as I waited for the elevator. She'd gone into the glass office at the end of the corridor, she was talking with the on-duty nurse she'd already asked about the private room. Was she already trying again? I took that for a good sign. I managed to tell myself that it would pass very soon, that she'd sail through it, and then later, outside, after the big admissions desk, there was all that green on the trees, and I told myself that I didn't know how to pray. I had always been against praying.

I walked toward the Seine to have a quiet smoke. Turning around, I searched with my eyes for the ward where she was, without being sure. When I got to the riverbank, I ran across the road. They'd just demolished the apartment block where I'd spent the first years of my life, my mother having quickly stuck me with a sitter because she'd found a paying job. But there are some memories you can't demolish as easily as that. I lit another cigarette from the butt of the previous one and sat down on the grass, taking care to avoid the dog shit and all the garbage that was there. Beer cans, supermarket carts, debris from all over the world, and sometimes, toward the far end of Clichy, near the Île Saint-Denis, syringes that reminded me of Antoine, Marc-André's son, every time. I was under the poplars on the riverbank. They'd always been there for me, straight and clear, not saying anything, watching and waiting. Opposite, there were barges moored, and behind them, the building where Marco's parents had lived, when was it they'd died? I talked to Ben too. Did he have any idea of all the time I spent talking to him, almost every day, without telling him?

I didn't feel like going back to Marie's place that evening. She'd have liked me to live in her apartment, she was worried about security and she was also scared of missing important messages. She didn't want to tell her patients that she'd be unavailable for a few months. She wanted to go back to work as soon as possible, they really needed her, she thought. Who needed me now? I decided to go back to my apartment, even if I went to sleep at her place afterwards. I often hoped that Ben would never love without being loved in return. At other times, I hoped a whole lot of other things for him. The Seine was heavy today. When

I stood up again, I decided to give him a ring to suggest we have a meal together, if he had time. They were going to move soon. The storage facility at the port of Genn-evilliers was another of those old memories I didn't cherish. Just after the divorce, I lived all over the place, and sometimes, later, Benjamin and I even spent the weekend in a furnished room rented by the month in Bécon-les-Bruyères, because I know the landlord. I filled out his social security statements and the papers for his accountant instead of him, to thank him. He could have been one of those guys walking up and down the boulevard near where Marie lived. Or else a guy like him. I always felt better after a good quarter of an hour near the Seine.

At home I waited until evening. I called my son but it was Anaïs who picked up, how are you?

"Yes, we're exhausted, we're still packing. Ben's in the basement, he'll call you back, OK?"

He called back ten minutes later, was I still on for the storage facility the following Saturday, was it all right with me? I said yes, preferably in the morning. Then I don't know how it happened, but we started talking about scooters, and he laughed, I'd been wanting one for so long, it might be better if I gave up the idea, unless maybe I waited until winter? That was what decided me, I think. That and all these other complicated desires to go around the old places I'd known in my life. It wouldn't take me more than ten minutes to get to Beaujon if I had a scooter. To get to the office, I could always park near the railroad station at Pont Cardinet.

"How's Marie?"

"Not very well."

I heard him stiffen at the other end, he must have made a sign to Anaïs— oh, those irritable signs his mother made, I remembered them so well—what's wrong with her? She has breast cancer, I told Benjamin, she went into

Beaujon today for an operation. She should pull through. That was the phrase I'd heard more than once, it came to me like that without thinking. Benjamin was silent at the other end.

"Maybe we could meet before Saturday, if you like."

"Yes, if you like, how about coming to dinner?"

He whispered some things to Anaïs and then said no, we're busy, can you come here? That way you'll see the mess we have! Marie had switched off her cell phone. The message on it wasn't one she'd recorded herself, and since it bothered me that I hadn't been able to speak to her, I made a detour and went past Beaujon, just to wish her good night from the side where the windows on her floor were. I don't know why I had the impression that would help her without her being aware of it. After all, nobody would know apart from me, but anyway.

...

Marco did the same thing sometimes. When his son wasn't doing well, he'd go to the church at Porte de Champerret and light candles, like an idiot. He'd never set foot in there before he was forty, and he didn't tell anyone about it, not even Aïcha. Of course it hadn't cured Antoine of his addiction, he would always be an ex-junkie, with chronic hepatitis and a criminal record, but in his opinion it was thanks to the candles that he'd always had the courage to visit him in the hospital, in rehab, and at Fresnes prison, where his son had done six months, and to look him in the eyes. It was just a matter of finding places where guys like him and me could be alone and quiet for a moment, to do their black or white or blue or pink or whatever magic. I got to their place around nine in the evening. It was really nice to see them again, surrounded by all those boxes. When he came into the kitchen, Benjamin asked me to come and help him, and he told me that his mother had asked about me.

"Oh, yes?"

"Yes."

He was handsome, my son, with his curly hair tumbling over his forehead and his eyes still like a child's, despite his job in the labs in Switzerland, and maybe later, in the United States. By the time he finished studying, he'd be over thirty.

"And what did you tell your mother?"

"Oh, that you seemed to be OK."

"You said the right thing," I told Benjamin.

Do you mind if I pull down the curtain? The previous week I'd read in F. Scott Fitzgerald's biography that he had short legs and was a chronic alcoholic and full of hang-ups, one night when he was drunk he took Ernest Hemingway into the toilet of a bar and asked him to tell him if he was normally endowed, and Hemingway apparently did nothing to reassure him. He even told the story, which just goes to show. I should have taken more interest in books earlier in my life. After my divorce, and even in the last two years of our life together, I'd been incapable of concentrating on anything. We finished eating. Anaïs started piling up books and papers from her classes. The edge of each colored folder had the year written on it. She had no idea what she was going to do in Zurich. She seemed quite down. She had a new tattoo on her lower back, which had hurt a fucking lot, as she put it, do you want to see? Benjamin turned to me with a smile, what do you think? It was worth it, I said. Benjamin laughed and shrugged, it was a blue and black eagle with its wings spread. She had a new one done every year, for her birthday. This one had been a gift from Ben. I'd already seen some of them at the seaside in previous years. I didn't really know Anaïs well. They kissed, and suddenly the thought of Marie's illness hit me really hard, that shit.

I'd go past the hospital again this evening, I'd have to ask her what time she went to sleep, so that I could call her without disturbing her. We carried the heavy things together, we pushed them into the hallway. I was sweating like a pig. They'd have friends to help them at the storage facility in Gennevilliers but I was welcome to come, when was I going to the hospital? Visiting hours are in the afternoon, aren't they, could you come in the morning? No problem, yes, I'll come on Saturday morning. I got back in my car at midnight. Anaïs gave me the rest of the apple pie, that was nice of her. I left a message on Marie's cellphone. I missed her a lot that night. There was no one on my street. I found a parking space straight away. I had so many things to do now. I was scared I wouldn't manage. I fell asleep trying not to think about it, not to tell myself anything about Marie's illness, but there was no point trying, with guys like me. I remembered some very old things too, I dreamed about my childhood. That doesn't happen often these days. It seemed quite beautiful now. Why? Maybe because I didn't have much time left? And then finally it all calmed down, as if nothing had happened, just like that, because it was the next day.

The weather was really nice now. It was easier for me to get up in the morning. As I waited in the station for my train, I'd smoke a cigarette and go over what I had to do. My colleagues in the office were vaguely in the know, and I'd started getting there an hour earlier than them in the morning, but I'd leave on the dot to get to Beaujon. The whole time, it seemed to me that I was being followed, or spied on. Like with Larrieu, I'd run into him on one of the floors or on the street and he'd ask me how I was. Or else the girl on the switchboard, over the past few years I'd gotten into the habit of joking with her, and now she was openly ignoring me, as if I was in trouble with the law. I had to get a grip on myself. Nobody's interested in a guy like you, *old chap*. Anaïs had found the original expression in *Gatsby*, old chap. I hated that expression. But I was finding it difficult to put on a brave face in the office. I made a few mistakes, and on two occasions, a file I'd approved came back onto my desk, after going up three floors, with a post-it and some initials in red. I mustn't fall behind, they didn't say anything but there were a number of guys like me they were waiting to see make mistakes.

When I left work, I wouldn't stop to have a beer or a coffee in the bar at the end of the street, the way I used to, I'd go straight to Brochant on foot. I'd walk in the company of the trees as far as the darkness on the ground floor of Marie's building, to pick up her mail. The operation had gone well but she was extremely tired, quite apart from the treatment she was starting. She was worried, how was she going to stand it? Some friends of hers had painted a picture of it that terrified her, plus, what made her sad was seeing all these people alone in life, apparently. How to find the strength to get out of their ward in the hospital, to go where?

Two days after the operation, I went to help Benjamin put his things in storage. I stayed in the locker he'd rented at the port, I arranged the things as best I could to fill the space. Anaïs had marked all the boxes: their departure was very well organized. His mother and I had lived in Gennevilliers for two years, in my head it was still a place where I'd dissipated my youth, along with a few other places in the Hauts-de-Seine, with Marco most of the time. In the aisles of the storage facility, Africans with rap in their ears and sometimes betting slips from the horse races in their hands made the rounds, I also saw dogs with their handlers in the aisles. Behind the row of birches on the edge of the site, you could see the high fence of the port, and beyond that, a whole heap of places whose names I couldn't remember, but which I'd crisscross as soon as I had my scooter and Marie had recovered as I hoped she would. I could take photographs. They'd gone back to load the J7 with the last boxes and my son had suggested I wait for them, Anaïs had left with him. Right, so we'll see each other at the airport, then? She and I had kissed and I'd realized that it was almost as if I was grieving, in a small way, but it probably wouldn't be the last time.

They took almost an hour to finish loading and come back. I was exhausted after the last two weeks, dividing my time between the office, Beaujon, Marie's apartment, and mine. That was why I didn't look at myself too closely in the mirror, in the morning or at night, because I wasn't too curious to know what I looked like at such moments. Probably another guy like me, *old chap*. He was really fascinating, that man. He was a poor guy from the sticks, and when he reached the bright lights, he started to have his doubts, things weren't any better here than there. He messed up his life, without meaning to. There were probably millions like him on both sides of the ocean. Who could I talk to about that? Marc-André and I had supported each other quite a bit on the phone lately. His son had lost ten pounds in a month since he'd stopped his treatment. Marco was scared that he'd go back to his habit. Marie was very anxious, and Benjamin's leaving was weighing on my mind. I still bore just as much of a grudge against my life, in a way. For many years, you had to fight against the sensation of living for nothing, and then, when you thought you more or less knew why, the reason could disappear like that, and you realized you'd been tricked. How could you get over these things? Of course, Marco knew all this as well as I did and he didn't have the answer. Neither did I. When can we meet? We asked each other that every time. I'll call you when I can.

Aïcha always asked me to give Marie her regards, and then we'd call each other again two or three days later, to chat. The trips to Beaujon were starting to get on my nerves. I realized that one evening on my way there: since the birth of my son, I'd only ever set foot in there for bad news, a stay in the hospital when I was fifty, and two deaths.

Marie read a lot. When I arrived, she was often also asleep. As soon as she was able to get up after the operation, she started taking care of herself, she put on make-up, she didn't want to let herself go. I went to the cosmetics department of Printemps with a tube of lipstick, she wanted me to find the same one. I liked doing that a lot. She'd put on perfume, she could still stand Chanel No. 5.

"I don't smell of illness, do I? You wouldn't lie to me?"

Her girlfriends came to see her almost every day. I'd already seen some of them at her place, she'd talked about them for months on the internet, the others too, now I'd see them arriving with flowers or candy. When they left Marie would give it all to the nurses, and to the nurses' aides who cleaned the corridors and the wards. Little by little, seeing her living like that, almost furtively, I told myself that she was a real chance for me. She'd received a postcard from Benjamin and Anaïs. Show me, did you really? She would have to stay here almost another month, for short periods. Later, there would be outpatient radiation therapy, and then it would be over, that was what everybody hoped. Sometimes we actually managed to be alone for a while, she and I. She didn't know what had happened to the young woman she'd seen when she first came. It had been really depressing, hearing her get up at night, call for help in a low voice, then go and spew her guts out. In Beaujon, so close to the Seine, so close to where Marco and I both lived, you were already far from other people, from life as it goes on.

One time, I told Marie that when Benjamin was born I'd gone down to the emergency room to phone my parents who were asking for news. A hairy young guy buttonholed me, he wanted to scrounge a little money from me, I told him to leave me alone, I had other things on my mind, I'd just had a child! He gave me a crooked smile and said: you've just had a kid and you don't even want to stand me a drink to celebrate? He turned around, genuinely disgusted. I'd never forgotten that, though I didn't really understand why it had made such an impression. Do you mind if I pull down the curtain? Benjamin knew that story by heart, he'd always listened to it politely, as if to say, why did that memory matter so much to me?

"You should have had a drink with him," Marie said, "that way you wouldn't have thought about it anymore."

Then she asked me to sit down next to her and we stayed like that for a while, looking toward the other bank of the Seine. She didn't feel too bad. Most of the time she didn't feel anything. She spent her time not feeling anything. She was waiting. It was too hot in Beaujon. The last days of April and the first days of May, I was pleased that month was coming, with its long weekends and its public holidays. I was exhausted. I've never in my life been good at doing lots of things at the same time.

When I left Marie, she was tired.

"Do you need anything?"

She summoned up the courage to smile, and I don't think she was faking it. Well, maybe sometimes.

"Yes, I need you to get rid of my cancer, could you do that for me?"

She never asked me to leave. Whenever I went, she would turn her head toward the window of her room, sometimes she had to put on her sunglasses, and it was if she was waiting her turn in a detox center or something like that. But we were out of luck. All I could do was tell myself crap like that. I looked on the internet two or three times, I bought magazines with articles about breast cancer, but there were never any answers to the questions I asked myself. They were irrelevant, obviously. What did she think about during all those hours of waiting? Everything and nothing. She tried above all not to ask herself too many questions, she told me she was trying to stop wondering why. "Why" kills faster than any other word.

The doctors had told her she would lose her hair. She didn't know when. She didn't want to wait. She was going to have her hair shaved off and buy herself a wig the following week, when she left the hospital. I offered to come with her, but she wouldn't hear of it. She wanted to hear about the Brasserie Wepler, or for me to tell her about the boulevard, the trees on her street, she missed that, her life, her friends, her neighbors, and all those people she met in the clinic, her love of the night people, as she called them. She unwittingly came out with these grand but simple phrases. Damn Mr. F. Scott Fitzgerald, *old chap*. We hadn't led the same life at all, she and I. They kept her in for a few more days after the first chemo, to see how she reacted. Then they let her go. Marie didn't have any family, she'd dumped them the day she turned eighteen, but that didn't mean she was alone. I liked seeing her surrounded by her girlfriends, and when I was there, they all looked at me in the same way, they all gave me the same slightly vague, slightly fake smile, a bit like, when you're hiring, you smile at the applicant as you ask him to sit down. But I was probably just imagining things.

...

I'd forgotten all about him. Marco heard from him from time to time, they weren't calls for help, although not far off, but he didn't see what more he could do for him. In any case, in his opinion, strange as it might seem, Jean had never really wanted to get back to work. He talked to him mostly about Adeline Vlasquez. He really would have liked to find her again. He was also thinking about his mother in Marseilles. How old was she now? Marco and I both remembered the concierge's lodge where we sometimes went to pick him up. Every year it was a little grayer in our memories when we talked about it. Maybe one day the color wouldn't even exist anymore? It was a bit further away also. But when it came down to it, he'd only left it temporarily, he was back on the ground floor looking out on a courtyard. He'd been born like that. He hadn't really suffered from his childhood, or maybe he couldn't talk about it? Marco would ask me how Marie was and I didn't know what to reply. Her illness was bringing her and me closer together. I had the feeling I'd known her for a very long time. Whenever she thought she was alone, she'd look out of the window of Beaujon, at the other side of the Seine, with her sunglasses. Do you mind if I pull down the curtain? It was too hot in the wards. There were fans in the corridor, which were almost no use at all.

Once or twice we slipped out because she wanted to smoke a cigarette, which was completely forbidden because of what she had.

"You won't do it again, will you?"

Marie smiled at the nurse who came rushing to us as we stood by the elevators. In the end, the nurse shrugged and told her not to stay up too long, and then I left. Marco asked me casually what would happen when she finally left the hospital, and then when she had finished her treatment and recovered?

"We haven't talked about it yet, I don't know."

I could tell he was smiling on the other end.

"What are you doing? Are you still there?"

"It's been a long time since you were last in love, if you

don't mind me saying so."

"Oh, really? Is that true?"

He laughed softly, of course it was true. I realized that yes, it was true. In the end, I'd only waited twenty years for Marie. We had to stop talking on the phone, we had to see each other at least. Otherwise life soon became nothing.

"Wait, I'll have a look."

Marco whistled as he suggested dates. Apart from my evening visits to Brochant and to the hospital, I was alone, the dates were all the same to me, and I didn't really mind. Quite the opposite. I was pleased to realize it, we'd meet on Friday. Should I come to his place? Aïcha was leaving for another conference in Marseilles, we could eat out if you like?

I took my son and Anaïs to the airport. We were in the terminal, they'd already left in a way, we had no more time to lose. They'd spent the last night at my ex-wife's, she hadn't been able to get away, she would go to see them, but she didn't yet know when. It would have been easier if after our separation we'd learned to talk, but we hadn't. We'd been at each other's throats for years. He gave me their temporary address, Anaïs was at a newsstand buying some magazines. At first they'd be staying with a colleague who was also from Paris, they didn't have anywhere to live yet. I really would have liked to tell my son a few things at that moment, as if we were never going to see each other again, as if I was going to leave before them. Instead of which, we chatted as if he would be there the following weekend. He'd given me a little digital camera and had showed me how it worked, we'd both laughed and made faces, these last few days, between his lab and the office.

I don't like airports. It's never guys like me who are leaving, I'm one of those who stay. After a while, we're even the only ones who remember, and nobody much seems to care. My son … yes, my father? He talked like that when he was twelve, we always spoke to each other in the same way.

"My son will set the table."

"Has my father made pasta again?"

I was filled with those words, and what else did I have, when it came down to it? The three of us went out to have a smoke before they left and there was a lot of noise.

"By the way." Ben gave me a little package. "Here it is, open it when we're gone, OK?"

"For me? What is it?"

Anaïs was laughing and I put it in my pocket without having the slightest idea.

"It's nothing, a trifle."

I must have made a funny face, I guess, but I don't know. They'd be in touch within a week, what the hell would they be able to do in that idiotic country? Eat fondue? Go skiing in winter? Carry suitcases full of fake banknotes? They weren't really happy to be leaving, but in an hour, if I knew them, they would have decided once and for all and Ben would keep it to himself. We went back into the concourse. Anaïs moved away to make a phone call, Ben looked at her two or three times out of the corner of his eye. Is everything all right, my son?

"Yes. She's really down. Leaving her mom and dad and her friends, plus she can't find a job … You know how it is."

I wondered if he hadn't become a guy like me at that moment, watching her as she phoned home. Do you mind if I pull down the curtain? No, father, what about you? My son, let's open it gently and look together at the landscape, I really wonder what this place is where we've landed. Are you all right? Yes, yes. I opened one eye. Your turn. It's hard to see, but wherever we go, I'm fine. Then we had to say goodbye.

They were already on the plane when I realized I hadn't

managed to tell them I loved them, as I would have wanted-
ed. I hoped that, in the end, he'd never become a guy like
me. He'd been lucky, he'd left in time, he'd gotten away
from all that, at least I hoped so. I could feel the little
package in my jacket pocket. I paid for the parking time
at a machine, and then I noticed that I had lost my car, I
went crazy, it took me a good quarter of an hour to find it
again, in parking garage B2. I hadn't forgotten which row
it was in, I'd simply gotten the wrong floor, well anyway.
As I was leaving, just after I went through the gates, a
plane took off just above my head, I closed my eyes without wanting to. I took my time going home. I felt sad and
happy, as we all are, I'm talking about guys of my type,
there are only a few million of us, I think.

I'd never been able to talk to his mother again. Ben has
suffered a lot from that, I think. She sent the bailiff to
me twice in a row, during a period of unemployment and
depression, I've never forgiven her. All I could do was not
let anything pass that would embarrass Benjamin, I don't
even know if I managed that at least. We've never talked
about it directly. Marco knew these things by heart, he'd
held my head above water for months. I'd also been lucky,
when you think about it. With the years, all the words I
reserved for her had been drained of their meaning, and
even the features of her face had gradually lost their sub-
stance. The things I could have blamed her for, the failure
of our marriage, none of it meant anything to me now.
There was a big hold-up near Bondy on the A3, and then
another one on the beltway. I found a parking spot under the trees at Louise Michel. It was pleasantly gray on
my street. I lowered the blind in the living room and lay
down on the couch, I tried to reason with myself but I'd
had enough of being reasonable and I let myself go, it did
me a lot of good.

But because of that, I looked really terrible in the bath-room mirror. I took a shower, as I usually do in such cases. I changed. Then I opened Benjamin's little package, it was a child's toy. He'd been ten years old. Maybe I was already dreaming of a scooter. It was his old red Vespa made out of scrap iron, I'd completely forgotten it. But he'd carried it around with him in his pocket for a good couple of years, as if he was saying to me, one day we'll both have one when I'm big. OK? Only it was all worn, the color had gone on the wheels and the handlebars. I looked for a place where I wouldn't lose it. I put it on my desk, just under the lamp. I sat down in front of it. I remembered those things. And that was it.

· · ·

In the days that followed, I went to the office early. The weather was quite good. It was a pleasure to leave early, carrying my jacket over my shoulder. Sometimes it seemed as if I'd spent a long night, and the rest of the time I never stopped remembering. Marie and I hadn't talked any more about the summer, in theory, around July, she would have a few days' respite between chemo sessions, and if it was OK, she'd be able to leave. She had a friend in Trouville, who had a house by the sea. She could let us use it. Do you know Trouville? Yes, I've been before, I really like it there. I'd planned my vacation for July, one week, and an-other week in August, since Ben had stopped going away with me I'd always taken them in installments, because what would I have done with all that time, on my own, with nothing to do? He called me a week after his arrival, Anaïs was happy, she'd already found a part-time job … As for him, he wasn't sure yet. I didn't go to see Marie every evening. She was starting to be exhausted by it all. She'd started losing her hair after the second session, and she'd thrown up a lot. When they let her out, I saw her home. She wanted to ask them for a break from therapy, but they wouldn't let her. She'd see about it later, when she felt better. She was happy to be going home for a few days. I'd only been to Brochant to air the place out and pick up her mail, a girlfriend of hers from the boulevard also dropped by sometimes.

"Home at last!"

She was in a good mood, and we went for a meal at the Brasserie Wepler. She only picked at her food, to be honest, but she had a wonderful auburn wig now, she looked stunning. She was also happy to see the boulevard again: it was still just as ugly, noisy, and gray, all the way to Brochant metro station.

Several times I felt her looking at me out of the corner of her eye. In the end, I asked her what it was she wanted to tell me and couldn't, or was I imagining things? No, I wasn't imagining things. She'd have liked to be less tired and to show me another side of herself. She'd had too much time to think when she was in Beaujon. She'd never wanted to live with a man, not in a long time anyway. But we could see each other, if she wasn't too tired. In the evening, she cried a lot because she'd been very happy and very unhappy in her life, and she accepted that, but today she was scared that she wouldn't see the rest of it. She needed some time alone, she said.

"We have plenty of time ahead of us, Marie."

It came out without thinking. She looked at me without a word, do you really believe that? And I was so sure of myself at that moment, in a way I'd rarely ever been in my life. So then she even wanted to go to the movies, just as she had hundreds of times, but there were too many people waiting in line, too many dumb films. It was hard for her to bear the noise and the gasoline smells. We walked back from the square to her apartment in Brochant, would I like a drink? No, thanks, I'm fine. So we just lay there in her bedroom, and then, when she was very tired, I left to go home and sleep. See you tomorrow?

"Yes, of course."

"Can you let the phone ring twice so that I know you've arrived?"

"Sure. Call if you need me, will you do that?"

"Yes, sleep well."

6

THERE HE WAS, WITH HIS VERY BLUE EYES, STANDING BY the boxes. He hadn't finished, but almost. The window was open, like the first time I'd paid him a visit. The window of the apartment opposite was closed. I don't know why I remember that family so well, is it because of the two children? He'd already packed the boxes. His rolling tobacco on the carpet, which was gray like the carpets in offices that haven't been rented yet. Stains. Marks from the feet of the table, where he must have spent hundreds of hours waiting, without finding. He'd closed the door, I'd simply given it a push to come in, calling out: are you there?

"Come in, it's nice of you to drop by."

I was a bit surprised because we'd agreed to meet, all three of us, to have dinner. His sense of humor was a bit of a problem sometimes, in his life. I watched him scotch-tape the boxes with great skill. He'd never been comfortable with words, but things like that he could do well, overcome that kind of difficulty. He didn't have many possessions. At a certain point, the window opposite half-opened and he took the opportunity to look up and offer me some tobacco. Just then, the image of his mother came back to me. He really did look like her, suddenly, lifting his head. How old had we been then?

"Do you want one? Help yourself."

I rolled myself a cigarette. He had a few ready-made

filters in the pack, but I didn't even try to put one in. He approached the window with a big smile. It was the same little boy as last time. He climbed over the sill and came in to take a look. Our eyes met for a moment.

"So you were at home, Akim? Are you OK?"

The boy nodded. "Where are you going? Are you going a long way?"

I recognized some things from when his mother had been a concierge.

"I'm going to Marseilles. By the way, tell your father to drop in, is he around now?"

"I don't know, he never says where he is. I'll tell him if I see him."

I sat down on the radiator under the window.

"Good, I'll do the rest later, what time's Marc-André coming?"

He still had some pastis, if I wanted. Yes, why not? Without daring to admit it to myself, I was almost impatient for the evening to end, this thing that didn't mean anything, from way down in our past. The kind of thing veterans do, except there hadn't been a war. There had simply been a life together, side by side in the Hauts-de-Seine, so many years on the streets of Asnières, Gennevilliers, Clichy, and La Garenne, and then, for each of us, love affairs, plans for the future, successes and failures, but he, in a way, had specialized. I couldn't help smiling to myself, thinking about it. He looked in the closet, then in the refrigerator, which he was leaving behind for whoever came after him, if there was anybody. It would only be a temporary lease, obviously, they were going to demolish everything around here. There was also the TV set, which he'd bought quite cheap, but it worked perfectly, he'd give it to the children opposite. He liked the idea of giving them a present. He wouldn't need it now. Oh, really?

"Yes, my mother has one, and anyway I don't like it."

"I'm like you, I never watch it."

He took the bottle of pastis from the almost empty closet. Sorry, I don't have any ice. He seemed to enjoy putting on this performance for me, as if he hadn't felt so happy to be alive in years. He rolled himself a cigarette too. His things piled up in the middle of the room, like the last possessions of a guy who's about to disappear.

The watch on his wrist drew my attention: it was an old watch, I'd seen watches like that a long time ago, on the wrists of uncles and neighbors during my childhood. He saw what I was looking at, it was my father's last watch, he said. He'd gotten nothing from him except beatings, in his early years. He'd been very happy when he'd left, when he was about ten, and so was his mother. He was smiling as if to himself. It occurred to me that this wasn't the first time he'd told this to someone. Then, when he died, in some little town in Brittany, it was a long time since they'd heard from him, either his mother or him. Anyway, he'd gotten his watch, a few photos, his mother had never wanted to tell him who the woman was beside him in the photographs. In any case it was working well.

"They made things properly in those days."

He said it as if it was a joke, and I had to smile again. He looked less weary than usual. He seemed happy to be leaving, I think.

"How about you? How are you?"

I'm fine, life's the same as usual. What could I really talk to him about? Marie? Of course not. He was one of those guys you can't imagine living for a long time with a woman, but who was I to think that of him? I told him that my son had gone away for six months for his work …

"Your son, oh, yes, what's his name again?"

"Benjamin."

He nodded, with a big smile. He remembered the christening well, at Sainte Odile, near the Porte de Champerret. I haven't seen him since, he added. Does he look like you? Then, having shot his arrow, he put his almost spent cigarette back in the corner of his mouth without waiting for my answer.

"Could you help me, please?"

By the time Marco arrived, we were taking out plastic bags filled with garbage, things to throw away, unusable things he'd amassed in this apartment. He'd always recycled, even when he wasn't obliged to. You surrounded yourself with tons of things without knowing, and it was always the same, with each move you had a big spring cleaning. Marc-André waved to us and took out his cell phone, he had an important call to make. We finished transporting what he had to throw away into the courtyard of the building. The kids opposite were looking at us, kneeling on the couch, the TV set on behind them, although they weren't looking at it. We could also hear the noise of the boulevard in La Garenne-Colombes where we used to walk together, all those years ago. It was still us, it wasn't really our home any more. Marc-André was standing in the doorway of the inner courtyard.

"Hi, how are you? Why don't you have the light on?"

We shook hands. "Fine, and you?"

"Not bad. One more day gone. Right, shall we go?"

He hadn't had time to give it any thought, and Jean didn't know the local restaurants. Maybe we could take the car and go to the big pizzeria in Clichy? It wasn't far from Beaujon, on the way back I could go there and look at the windows on her floor. Was I more superstitious than before? What were we really afraid of, time rushing by and taking us to our end? Marc-André was looking around.

"So, this time it's true, you're really going for good?"

"Yes, this time I've had enough, I'm leaving."

He smiled as if admitting defeat. And yet it seems to

me something was driving him and it wasn't his failure, on the contrary, it was a desire to leave, a desire to be somewhere else, that was stronger than him. Somewhere else?

"I think it's better this way. And besides, my mother's eighty-two, I want to take advantage of the time she still has, you know."

Marco looked tense. Several times lately, he'd told me he was fed up with his success. He was too tired to want any more of it. But he spoke about it with Aïcha, and then everything became possible again, because he was no longer alone in this life. You had to accept that there was a price to pay. Guys like him didn't get anything for nothing, when it came down to it, that was the case with most of us. I got in the back seat of Marc-André's car.

There were two red lights in succession, and we didn't say anything, all the time we sat there waiting. Guys with their windows down, their radios on or their cell phones in their hands, waiting for the lights to change. He held himself very straight, at one moment our eyes met in the rearview mirror. Marco turned to me.

"I'm fed up with these hold-ups. By the way, what about your scooter, do you have it?"

"Soon, yes."

Jean turned to me. "Don't you already have a car?"

He smiled vaguely, as he often did. When we got to Clichy, a car was just pulling out and we didn't have to drive around looking for a parking space. Marco got out first, he switched off his cell phone. That way I can have a little peace and quiet. I've had a rough day. We sat down in the smoking area. The place had been refurbished two years ago and, in addition to the music, which was a little too loud, the lighting was also too harsh in the middle of the room. We sat down in a corner at the far end. Jean had brought his case with him. When they took our orders and served the aperitif, he told us he wanted to show us some photographs, to see if they reminded us of things. I thought that was weird, Marco was as surprised as I was. He'd kept everything. It was still in his case, he had never let it out of his sight. He'd stuck some of them in a school notebook, along with the dates, sometimes followed by a question mark. The oldest dated from 1976. The three of us were twenty, barely more than children. I recognized some of them, class photographs I must have somewhere at home, then he showed us others in which we didn't appear.

Several photographs in the courtyard of the building where he lived with his mother. He had the same eyes as her, the same way of looking with a slight lift of the head, the way people look under their glasses, except that he didn't wear glasses. Photos also of him when he was very small, that was my father, he said, pointing to a middle-aged man, who really seemed to be from another time, very distant even in the 1970s, and even further from us today. And then lots of photographs taken in Asnières, at the Bar des Trois Communes, where we sometimes went, and at Nazim's in Bois-Colombes, the one who had died only two months ago and had had a good life. We really had lived it up. We gradually relaxed. We even pushed away our plates, there was a kind of fire still burning in all this that went beyond our common memories. When the waitress brought us our meals, we left his photographs to one side. We told each other about long-gone things. There were our teachers and our parents. The injustices never swallowed, the hopes never followed by results. Then there were the stories about girls, love affairs we'd never forgotten. We realized we'd pretty much known the same girls in high school, and at Le Cercle near the station, we spent a whole lot of time there, and when we were alone, up until the early '80s, that was where we went. Generally, you didn't have to wait too long.

He was getting excited as he spoke, our memories were gradually falling into place, just like that, for no reason, he was putting our past together. We ordered a good bottle of red wine, we had to celebrate this, in the end it had been a good idea of his to make us revisit our lives. There weren't so many of us left now. We'd lost touch. And then almost nobody lived in our old neighborhood in the Hauts-de-Seine anymore. He had other photographs in a small brown envelope. Several times, he seemed hesitant to show them to us.

"Here, I have this too, if you want. I'll be back."

He went to the toilets. Marco watched him walk away and shook his head.

"Are you thinking the same as me? I'm surprised he held out all this time."

I opened the envelope. It was her, the girl he'd been harping on about all this time. Adeline Vlasquez. She was wearing a long flowered skirt on platform B of the station at Asnières, and in the sunlight the colors looked a little fake. They were already old, these photographs. In this one, he had long hair, he was wearing a shirt with a large collar, he had his arm around her shoulders and they seemed to be in love. Who'd taken the picture? Do you remember this girl? I had only a vague image of this Adeline Vlasquez.

"He's in a bad way, though, I wonder how he's going to pull through this time."

I put the photos back in the envelope. He came back toward us with a big smile.

"Did you look at them?"

"Yes," we said. "They're great. That was quite a time. Do you still hear from her?"

He'd looked for her for a long time, and in his opinion, all these last few years he wouldn't have let himself go the way he had if he'd been able to keep track of her, which was pointless, since she hadn't chosen him. Marco was looking around him, and then after a while he took off his glasses and massaged his eyelids.

"And what are you going to do now?"

"I'm going to see my mother, didn't I tell you?"

"Yes, but what are you going to do to earn a living?"

He shrugged. "I'd really like some dessert. How about you?"

We talked about other things. We were relieved that he'd finished showing us photos of his life, and also the life he thought had been ours. He seemed quite happy, though, that evening. But I couldn't be sure. Not far from here, there was this woman who might become mine, I hoped that very strongly, and I didn't know why, and then there was my son in Switzerland who called me from time to time. He'd suggested we contact each other via instant message. Whenever I got home, I switched on the computer and looked to see if he was online. He had a lot of work. I wrote more often to Anaïs, she'd started taking German classes, she'd be coming back to Paris from time to time, she hadn't yet decided what she was going to do. We stayed in the pizzeria for a long time. Maybe we wouldn't have many more opportunities? Marco would have liked to stop working, he was earning a good living, but it didn't matter anymore, Aïcha was advising him to do what he wanted, but what did he want? Over time, he'd forgotten what he liked. For lots of guys like us, nothing mattered anymore. He would have liked to do legal counseling for people with money troubles, defend widows and orphans, instead of which he handled corporate accounts, surrounded by guys … Jean was listening to us and smiling, as if we'd thrown a great party just for him. It was coming to its end now.

I found it sad, when I got home that night, but not really, it wasn't as sad as all that, to be honest. You just have to let yourself go from time to time. It doesn't lead to anything, with guys like us. He hadn't wanted us to drive him home. How was he going to manage with all those boxes? Oh, he'd ask Ahmed, the neighbor opposite, to lend him his station wagon. We weren't too worried about him. In any case, he'd try to be in touch before he left for Marseilles.

"Can we do anything for you?"

"For me?"

For a moment, he seemed troubled.

"No, but I'll let you know where I'm living. We should keep in touch, don't you think?"

We shook hands. His handshake was too strong. The son of the concierge where we'd taken root, the lover of Adeline Vlasquez, the girl in the flowered dress on platform B of the station. The man who'd never managed to … Our friend too, in the end, who kept traces of our lives in a case, the same as all those guys who pretend that things are normal, when in fact they aren't. His mother would be happy to see him again. He picked up his case. Thanks for dinner. Right, shall we go?

He strode along Boulevard Jaurès, in the direction of the bridge, we let him go, the way guys like him do. His life wasn't slowing him down tonight. He seemed impatient to leave. He'd never really been there with us, but he remembered everything, he'd carried our memory in that case along with the welfare papers, the forms, and the discount vouchers. He was probably going to come back into our lives, but when? Marco and I were still watching him. He was walking quickly, like a man much younger than he was, surrounded by the lights of the Seine.

"Why did he want to see us, because of the photos? He doesn't want us to help him. Can you understand that?"

"I don't know, why not?"

We couldn't see him anymore now.

"Aïcha isn't in this evening, shall we have a last drink?"

We walked on the other side, along the same boulevard, as far as Porte de Champerret.

We talked a bit more about him. There'd been times, of course, when we'd wanted to know about him, it was true that he'd always been there, when we were teenagers, and those good years we'd had before that, it was strange when it came down to it. People were chatting calmly in the café. I'd seen Marc-André in this very place, the evening after my divorce. The big bus station is opposite, where you catch buses for the suburb I've never left. How about you, are you OK? Yes, fine. His son was a little better, he was feeling depressed, because of the pills. He'd be sick all his life. Now he was reading tons of books. He might go to college after all. He wanted to become a teacher but he didn't know if he'd be able to, especially as he had a criminal record. Marco was sometimes afraid of disappointing Aïcha, not living up to expectations.

"What expectations do you mean, Marco?"

But I understand that kind of fear, I have it too, obviously. We smoked like young guys and still drank too many beers. He was there between the two of us, that night, as he hadn't been in a long time. Of course, we'd wondered what had become of him, but our lives probably kept us too busy for us to really look for him. Do you mind if I pull down the curtain?

We also talked about Marie. This time, she had to spend five days in Beaujon. It's not going too badly, as well as it can, I told Marco.

"How many sessions does she have left?"

"They changed the treatment plan, they've added two."

And then, after that, there was the radiation therapy. We left. We'd meet again soon. There weren't many
people at Porte de Champerret. There was only the night
bus circulating now, the one with the owl, but only one
per hour, so I walked home. No message on the answering machine. It was two in the morning, I didn't feel like
sleeping. Marie preferred to be alone on nights like this.
I understood, I mustn't rush her. There were times when
she was very tired, but all in all she was holding up well,
I thought. She read to pass the time. I'd lent her the F.
Scott Fitzgerald books, she'd made a face at first because
he was American and these days too many things in life
were American, but in the end she liked his work. *Tender
is the Night.* It isn't always like that. All the same, I'd had
a good evening. If I had time, I'd go see him again, would
he contact us before he left for Marseilles? When we were
teenagers, we'd dreamed of Marseilles. Or else, like when
he was a student, you could go to England or the United
States, how long was it he had stayed there? Maybe he really didn't need help, in the end. Maybe that wasn't what
he needed? I was already hung-over by the time I went to
bed and I couldn't stop swallowing, with all the cigarettes
I'd smoked. I'd have to quit again. At that moment, I felt
very old. I also felt alone, and so I was a little scared, I
think.

• • •

The next morning, I had two espressos at the Gare Saint-
Lazare, in the bar between the arrivals hall and the departures hall. I looked at myself in the window of Delaveine's
shirt store and I looked gray and grouchy. Nobody said
anything at the office, I worked without thinking. You
keep going without knowing, when it comes down to it. I
called Marie around noon and she was pleased to hear my
voice. She'd slept well during the night, but she had cold

sweats at times. Did you tell the doctor? No, she could
wait, she knew what it was anyway.

"Shall I drop by this evening?"

The weather was really nice when I got to Place de
Clichy. I liked stopping to look at the books, and sometimes, when she'd felt up to it, we'd gone back to look at
the people from the terrace of the Brasserie Wepler, which
is often worth it when you look at them from that spot. I
thought she looked beautiful among the other women. It
had to reflect well, somehow, on me and on all the guys
like me, when their lives start to seem like something. In
the evening I cooked, but she wasn't hungry at all, and
in the end, we spent most of the evening saying nothing,
sprawled on the couch. I liked it that way. She'd opened
the window and music was coming up from the inner
courtyard, which would usually have made her want to
dance, she said. She'd had visitors during the day.

· · ·

She wasn't alone like some people you saw getting chemo
in Beaujon. On the table she'd put the bunch of flowers
that some of the regulars from the boulevard had given
her, they had all signed a picture postcard of the Bati-
gnolles, her colleagues and her patients. It wasn't far away,
but it was a long way too, these days. She was tired of the
chemo. She was tired of not knowing, and of feeling her
body get rapidly weaker. She was tired of the cold sweats.
Plus, she was putting on weight, have you seen how fat
I'm getting? My eyes must have gone as round as marbles.
That made her laugh, and then she stopped. She was too
on edge. She didn't want me to see her in that state. She
asked me to forgive her. Don't talk nonsense, please. I'll
call you when I get home. Yes, I understand, don't worry.
Marie. I worked three more days. She really wasn't feeling
well, but it'll be OK, you can drop by later, don't worry.

"Why's everyone worrying? I'm not going to die to-morrow."

I wasn't very sure what I should do. On Friday I couldn't stop looking at my cell phone, it rang once but it was Benjamin, he wanted to know how I was. Anaïs was coming next week, oh, and how about the scooter? I hadn't done anything about it yet. Is something wrong? Marie isn't very well, I don't know, Ben. I thought to my-self that he was right about the scooter. I wasn't as alone as all that, when it came down to it, I would never be as alone as all that.

•••

Once, a year after the divorce, his mother had come to see me. I've never forgotten that, whereas if I met her again today I'd probably have the impression she was returning from another life, one where I could never take my place. We hadn't had any contact for a year. She'd had her lawyer send me letters, and out of the whole of our relation-ship, all I remembered now was the end, that anger I had against her, and she against me. Today, I've forgotten that anger. Why? I don't know. Was I already living in Leval-lois at the time? I can't remember, although it'd be easy enough to check. I hadn't yet left Asnières in my head, all my life I'd go to a lot of trouble not to move. But after only a few years, there was hardly anybody left I recog-nized, apart from Marco, obviously. She called me, she had something to tell me. I asked her where she wanted us to meet and she said, how about the café? We arranged to meet at the end of Rue de Rome, toward evening, af-ter work. We'd been regulars in that place. I'd even taken Benjamin there once, we'd just been to see a movie on Rue du Pasquier, in a theater I'd often gone to with his mother. I liked that theater, a long time ago. The female ushers were dressed in sky blue and lots of people came from the nearby suburbs. Ben was still all excited by the movie, was it *Star Wars*? I'm not sure. We had a Coke and everything I'd wanted to tell him, so that he'd know it and never forget it, I finally kept to myself. I got there early. I sat down to wait for her, and without meaning to I went over in my mind all the things she was going to blame me for, the times I was late bringing back Benjamin, the two months' alimony I hadn't paid, and that anger I felt, because I hadn't defended myself in order not to hurt my son, or even not to hurt us, the memories we had in common, and which are our only wealth, I think.

I thought she looked very beautiful when she arrived. Her hair was pulled back and her lips were very red, she'd never have worn that kind of lipstick when we were married. It suited her. She sat down opposite me, she was a little out of breath. Do you mind if I pull down the curtain? Well? She wanted us to make peace. She wanted us to be friends. That had to be possible between us. I sat there stunned all the time she spoke. I replied that it was weird, she was asking me this after a year of lawyers and notices from bailiffs, I'd only just found work again. She'd had no choice.

"We always have a choice," I said.

There are no second acts. Then we talked about Benjamin, since she wanted us to be friends. I would really have liked him to come on Friday evening straight after school, from time to time. Not just before noon on Saturday. There isn't much time, if you start at noon on Saturday. She never answered yes or no to this. She told me she would see. But it wasn't in the divorce settlement. So after a while, when she and I realized that we would never again be able to speak to each other, we sat there in that café without saying a word. How many couples had been there before us? How many couples who had thought they would love each other forever and had realized that in spite of everything it was all over? It was so commonplace, so why did we feel so bad? I felt as if I was in a boat swaying from side to side. But nothing is moving on deck. The filled glasses are emptied. The words burn for a brief moment, but as soon as the door of the café opens or closes they disappear, blown away by the wind. And in the end, when she leaves, or he goes out onto the street hardly able to breathe, with his eyes clouded over with nothing at all that you can name, not a single word of what has been said remains.

She stood up and searched in her handbag. She took out some cigarettes, she'd never smoked before.

"I'm seeing Ben next Saturday, is that right?"

I don't know if he ever knew she and I had seen each other. We never talked about it. Could I have been the friend she wanted? What was in it for me? I found myself in this same café after Benjamin's phone call. Why was it all coming back to me now, what I'd been through with his mother in this place fifteen years ago? That day, without knowing it, I'd signed up for years of not living. It had happened very quickly. Of course I hadn't realized it. After a few months on my own, I'd met some women, but we hadn't taken the time to get to know each other. It was like the empty words we'd spoken in that café at the end of Rue de Rome. Now I didn't want to lose Marie. I finished my beer and didn't waste time going all the way to Brochant on foot. She hadn't called me today and she hadn't answered my calls either.

I knocked several times at her door. I ran downstairs four steps at a time and asked the concierge for the key. I called the emergency medical service. I went with them from Brochant to Beaujon and they asked me what my connection was to her, but it didn't really matter. An intern came to see me after a while, it was an infection that had nothing to do with the illness, it happened sometimes, it wasn't serious. They were going to keep her in overnight, and tomorrow they'd see how she was and do some tests.

"Can I see her?"

They told me to wait while they got a room ready. They let me see her for five minutes, she had tubes in her nostrils and pills on the night table to be taken later, she had an IV in. She looked at me, we couldn't say anything to each other, and it was at that moment that I knew, I don't know why I knew but I knew, and I think Marie knew too, she was my second act. We held hands, without the words to tell each other this. She was looking deep into me, where I was the only guy like me at that moment. And there it was, and I left the hospital.

• • •

It was bright outside now, I didn't have to pretend anymore that I wasn't scared. I went back to the apartment in Brochant, I aired out the rooms, the smell of cooking came from the upper floor and made me feel good. There were always birds although there weren't any treetops around, I wondered where they came from. I felt like staying there for a while. We'd already spent a whole lot of hours like that, and in closing my eyes, I asked her the question. It was something like what the guy was asking in the F. Scott Fitzgerald book, when it came down to it, but I'd never found the right words in my life. It wouldn't be easy, with or without the illness. It had never been easy. I fell asleep. It was the dead of night by the time I got back home. The next day I finally bought my scooter. I got the salesman to explain everything, he was a young man the same age as Ben, he offered to take me for a spin. I also bought two helmets and a pair of gloves. I hadn't been on a two-wheeled vehicle since I was a teenager. But in the end it's just like a bicycle. I rode on the sidewalks in Levallois and people yelled at me, but what else could I do? I really think I was looking at everything in a new light. Was it a guy like me crossing at a red light, at a green? Where was he going? To his office? To see his family, to look for his memories? His mother in Marseilles or somewhere else? Was he alone that day? Had he always been alone? What were they all thinking about? There were so many places I wanted to go back to, I wanted to revisit my whole past. I quickly called Benjamin to tell him, he was fine, we'd speak soon on the phone. Two days later, Marie was already better. She didn't want to talk about what she'd had, it happened, and it might not be the last time. She wanted to go home, but the doctors didn't want her to, she was tired of it all, she was going to sign a discharge.

"Don't talk nonsense, Marie. What do you want me to bring you?"

"Do you still not understand? Something to get rid of the cancer, do you have it?"

"Marie, please. Calm down."

When she was angry, her eyes glowed very black, and she didn't look the same as when she was waiting on the couch thinking about things that didn't concern me.

After half an hour, a female resident came to see her, I had to wait outside in the corridor. We'd get through this together, the two of us. I was sure now. How is she? She's better. Don't stay too long, it tires her. Yes, thanks.

...

The scooter immediately changed my life. After my hospital visits, I wouldn't go straight home. I'd go for a ride, have a drink somewhere, in La Garenne-Colombes, or Bois-Colombes, or Asnières, or Saint-Denis, or Gennevilliers, often without any aim, just like that. There were places I'd never forgotten in Argenteuil and Sannois, where I had a girlfriend when I was a teenager, and also in Gennevilliers, where we spent quite a lot of time during our high school years. Marc-André also knew all these places. The others, where had they scattered to? I'd stop outside buildings that didn't have the answer. By the time I got home in the evening, I was happy to be there. I hadn't gone a long way, but somehow, it had been full of adventures, I told myself. They have nobody to get them into the flow of life, guys like me. So in the end their trajectories are like loops, they always have a tendency to retrace their steps. But that doesn't stop us from living, when it comes down to it. In the evening, after my day's work, I went back to the places I'd known as a child. I started taking photographs. I was leaving the office a little later now. That was because I wasn't sure of myself yet when I passed between the lines of cars that had stopped, waiting for them to start again. One evening after going to see Marie, I went back to La Garenne-Colombes, where he had lived before joining his mother. He hadn't been in touch yet. I parked just outside the entrance to his building, I felt like going inside to take a look. Not that there was anything of interest.

Everything around it had already been rebuilt, there were glass buildings and a lot of office space for rent, the cars were going fast along the expressway. There was nothing left to see around here. It wasn't the way it had been before. It would never be the way it had been before ... As for the building where he used to live, they must have been waiting for it to fall apart, and then they'd demolish it like the rest. Adeline Vlasquez, in the end I think I came back for her. The entry code didn't work, the lock had been forced. His name wasn't on the mailbox anymore. On top, there were some envelopes addressed to him, and I took them. Had he even notified anyone of his change of address or found someone to forward his mail? I pressed the button to turn on the light, and in spite of the noise from the expressway outside, you could hear it buzzing, just like when I was a kid, and also at my grandmother's house, a long time ago. A reminder letter from the phone company, a card from the electricity company saying their engineer had called, a few brochures, G20, Carrefour, Auchan, Celibaclub, a club for singles? Don't stay single anymore. A handwritten letter. A woman's handwriting, the name didn't mean anything to me. Should I take the letter or leave it with the bills? It would have been a bit of a headache, and besides, it was none of my business. I went into the inner courtyard. It had been raining that day. Behind the window, I saw the TV screen, the television was on, the kids seemed to be alone again, waiting for their parents. I knocked softly on the window pane.

"Hello, aren't your parents in? I came to see the neighbor."

"The neighbor Jean? The one who went to Marseilles?"

The kid looked back at the TV screen.

"Don't know, he left."

That was it, then. I said goodbye, and under my breath wished them a speedy departure too. I got back on my scooter. Honestly, how had I ever been able to live without it?

It's a straight shot all the way to Clichy, in twenty minutes, something like that. Just beyond the bridge is the Bar des Trois Communes, not far from the building where I lived more than forty years ago, which had only recently been demolished. I hadn't been in that area when it happened. I'd only seen the rubble. But here, on this section of the road to Asnières, nothing had changed, opposite the bar you still had the garage that rented old cars for movies, and the cobblestones had been poorly paved over, as if the asphalt didn't want to be there. One after the other, the buildings were boarded up, soon there wouldn't be a Bar des Trois Communes anymore. It was a bar of ill repute, a bar where nasty things happened, though of course nothing had ever happened to Marco and me there. On the wall facing the street, a pink marble plaque had been put up in 2000, engraved photographs of two young girls knocked down by a car, and there were flowers below them, a few bunches, to say that they would never be forgotten. I had always thought I wouldn't be forgotten either. But of course, everyone forgets. And sometimes it's better that way. I stayed there long enough to smoke a cigarette, I didn't go into the bar. There was a kind of war going on inside me, what had become of my life, and what could I do to change it? I calmed down, thinking about the good things that might still happen to me, but later it would be like the building where I spent my childhood or the Bar des Trois Communes, I was in no hurry to wait my turn but I wouldn't try to hide, the way children do.

I made a phone call before getting back on my scooter. Hard to believe I'd only just bought it, it was as if I'd had it my whole life, and I'd go traveling without moving from the Hauts-de-Seine and two or three arrondissements of Paris. Sometimes I slept at Marie's place, but most of the time I went home. I picked up her mail, watered the plants. I would stay there for a while, sitting on her couch in the empty apartment, daydreaming, hoping that we'd soon be living together, I really hoped for that. Plans for the future buzzed in my head at night, but the only way to deal with them was to go to sleep and keep them to myself. Too early? Too late? I couldn't decide. According to Marco anyway, I didn't have too much time left to let myself go. Aïcha had visited Marie in Beaujon, by the way. Oh, really? The four of us had only met once, the last time she'd come home after a chemo session. Marie wouldn't be moving into my place. With all that time ahead of me, I could start looking for a larger apartment, something to rent maybe, and I'd see if she liked it. Once or twice, when I started having my doubts, I took a shower, and another time, from the office, I called Benjamin and we spent quite a while chatting away. He was spending twelve hours a day in his lab. But do you like it? And what about Anaïs? Oh, so-so ... Bye, then. Speak again soon. Every week, we got in touch once or twice, and it had immediately become as important to me as the days when he came to me, when I'd go and wait for him outside school or at the end of the platform at Saint-Lazare, I would always wait for him anyway.

...

I'd had a drink with Marco the week before. He'd seen me coming on my Vespa and his face had lit up in a smile. He wanted to try it, but in our suburb it was better when there was nobody on the streets. At the office too, people laughed when they saw me. I was feeling more confident now and would go on long rides. We had a few days of rain, and then good weather again. Sometimes I'd set off blindly, or else a place from my past would come back into my mind and I'd decide to take a look at it. I must have been the old fool who only notices one thing, that whichever way you look at it, things aren't what they used to be. I kept these visits to myself, but gradually the idea came to me that I should tell all, that I should keep a record. Of course I didn't know how, or how long I'd do it for, I probably wouldn't have time to get to the end. I went back to his place, on the expressway. I'd hoped that someone would take care of his letters. They had boarded up the door and his windows in the meantime. The family who looked out on the courtyard hadn't left the place yet, but it couldn't be long now. When I arrived, they shut their window. What did they imagine? I didn't dare ask. There were more letters and reminders addressed to him, but what the hell, he'd been getting ready to disappear completely.

...

We did hear from him, the following month. He'd sent Marco a letter. He was pleased to be living in Marseilles. What beat everything was that he'd immediately found a job, luck often waits until the last moment. He was taking care of a large house with a garden and swimming pool in a ritzy neighborhood. It just goes to show, it must have been in his genes, taking care of a house. He had quite a lot to do, which he liked. The owners were German, but that was another story! He was living in a studio apartment away from the main house, and he took care of the maintenance, the gardening, he was starting to feel more self-confident. And then there was the sea and the sun. He went to see his mother once a week, she'd aged a lot, they'd diagnosed the onset of Alzheimer's. He should have gone earlier. His handwriting was clear and well rounded, as if he hadn't yet reached our age but had stayed the way he'd been before, in high school, when we were twelve or thirteen. When I went back to his last address on my scooter, the family across the courtyard had gone. The mailboxes had been torn off and someone had dumped hundreds of leaflets from a nearby supermarket. The entrance hall smelled of urine. That's it, I told myself, it's over. I did what I'd wanted to do the time before, or even a long time earlier to tell the truth. I took several photos with my little digital camera and returned home. In the evening, I went to Brochant. Marie and I went for a walk, as far as Place de Clichy, she wanted to see the new titles in the window of the bookstore. This time I saw two guys turn to look at her, and I think she noticed, so that was fine.

When we're together, we never talk about the future. I try not to talk too much about my past either, about all those years spent waiting for her, but well, you know guys like me. The doctors seem pleased with themselves anyway. We invited Marco and Aïcha to Brochant, I did the cooking, we had a good laugh, Marie was sick as a dog again the next day, but it isn't serious, she said. I took some photos too. I e-mailed them to Ben, saying look, it'll soon be September in Paris, isn't life beautiful? I wasn't completely drunk when I wrote that. Aïcha talked for a long time with Marie about the organization where she worked, they might be able to do some things together. Later, Marco offered me a cigar. We went out on the little balcony because it stank. We talked a little about him. Nothing to report, he said. He had a big smile. We were both happy that evening. We talked about the others we'd lost contact with. We both agreed that when it came down to it, everyone was alone, after a certain number of years. And then we smoked without saying anything, above the noises of the boulevard. I continued with my rides.

I sent Jean photos of our school, lots of places where we'd been, buildings, cafés. I'd gone back to the Bar des Trois Communes, at the end of the bridge on the border of Asnières. The plaque of the two little girls killed by a reckless driver, with the bunches of flowers below. The black cars with front-wheel drive in the garage opposite, and the slightly ridiculous limousines, fluorescent pink and petroleum blue, in an obscure corner of the suburbs, near the Seine. The demolished apartment block where I'd lived as a small child, which was probably the one that meant the most to Marco, because we'd both grown up there. He gave me back the photos and said: it's funny, I couldn't do that, it really tears me up. Doesn't it affect you? I realized it did, thinking about it. But it did me good, and besides, doing this, I wasn't idle when I wasn't at work, waiting for

Marie to recover completely. We came back with them. When they left, Marie asked me will you stay a while? We cleared the table and she started talking, she liked both of them, they seemed nice. Life could be normal every now and again. One last session to go, at Beaujon. She was scared every time. She was a little more scared, and she was expecting the worst. Or else, she'd completely forgotten and it was even harder to go back there. She didn't want to go back there, this evening. She didn't want to go to bed. She didn't want to. I said to Marie, I have an idea, are you coming? Let's go for a ride. I handed her a helmet, it was two o'clock in the morning. She'd ridden a motorbike before and she laughed because I'm not very expert. We took the Maréchaux toward Porte Maillot, it's the Way of the Cross for guys like me, and then we went to look at the Seine. We both love it. We were almost alone on the Pont Bineau. The reflections on the water were dark, almost proud, it seemed to be watching us, it was as if we could count on it and it would never abandon us. We parked on the sidewalk of the Pont Bineau. Marie held herself up against me, without saying anything, we turned north-east, toward Saint-Denis, it was funny how my whole life had been spent around that area, more or less. We looked in the direction of Beaujon too. It was a little cold on the bridge, so we went back. We couldn't keep from laughing. The following day, she got her bag ready at the last moment, and we went hand in hand to that horrible hospital, for the very last time, I swear. Oh, yes.

• • •

I went on with my life. Work, Marie in the evening, the photographs, the calls to Marco and my son. He was going to spend a few days in Jussieu and we decided we'd try to see each other. He was still just as badly dressed when

I went to wait for him that evening at the bus stop near Porte d'Orléans. We had a beer in a brasserie, he looked at my scooter and said, you certainly took your time! Anaïs sent her love.

"How is she?"

"Well ... not too bad. It isn't always easy, you know."

He was going to sleep at his mother's tonight.

"I brought the second helmet. Would you like me to give you a ride there?"

"Could you?"

"Sure," I said to Benjamin, "why not?"

He had a backpack and a small bag, I managed to wedge the bag between my legs, and he carried the backpack on his shoulders. I'll give you directions, OK? We headed north. We passed through the Maréchaux, it was easy to ride in the bus lane, so why hesitate? After a while, he tapped me on the shoulder and we turned right, she was living in Les Lilas now, she had an apartment there. We rode easily, at Porte des Lilas there was a van full of cops and I was sure they were going to arrest us, but they didn't. We drove up toward the park next to the water tower. It was another world, where Ben's mother lived. I parked on her street, not right outside the building, I tried not to think about all those trains I'd waited for at the Gare de Lyon and the Gare Saint-Lazare, and I think I managed.

"Shit," Benjamin said, "you certainly wouldn't win any races!"

I handed him his bag. He put it down on the sidewalk. I had my camera in my jacket pocket and he was standing in front of a large, more or less green willow, I felt like taking a photo. Really, he said, you want a picture of me? A guy was coming toward us. A tall black guy with headphones over his ears and huge sneakers.

"Excuse me," my son said, "could you take a photo of us?"

The guy shrugged and made a face like an actor when he heard what Ben was saying, without the headphones. We both struck a pose in front of the big willow on that little street in Les Lilas next to the water tower and he said are you ready, is your Dad going to smile? Good, how about another one? He seemed to be having a good time, taking our photo. We said thanks, no worries, he said, and he patted his chest next to his heart, the way people used to do, forty years ago, but it had gone out of fashion in the suburbs and then a few years ago it came back, so there you are. He strode off. We looked at the three photos he'd taken, they aren't bad, are they, I'll send them to you.

"When are you back again?"

"Next month, Anaïs and I are coming for a few days."

"We'll meet, right?"

"Can we crash at your place for one night?"

"Of course you can."

I put my camera back in my jacket pocket and he handed me the helmet. I put it away in the little compartment where I also keep a map of the suburbs of Paris. Sometimes, in the evening, I take it up with me and decide on the places I could go and revisit, places I used to go with my mother, with friends, because of girls, and sometimes for no reason at all.

"I guess she's waiting for you?"

He nodded. "Yes, it's number twenty-three."

He pointed to the little building where she lived. It was quite nice, I thought. Well, it wouldn't be long.

"Don't worry about it," I said.

He seemed to find it hard to leave this time. Earlier, in the café, he'd told me a bit about his life in Zurich. But that wasn't really it. He put on that look I knew so well and asked me just after we hugged: by the way, how's Marie? Marie's a lot better, I told Ben, she's coming out tomorrow. He gave me a big smile.

"Say hello to her from us, we'll see her next month, OK?"

"Yes."

At the intersection by the water tower I turned back towards him and he was still looking at me, he raised his hand. So did I. See you soon! He picked up his bag and turned right onto the little street where his mother lived. It wasn't bad around here, quiet, very green, just above the Bagnolet basin. I set off again, aiming for the Mercuriale towers at the junction of the A3 in order to get back on the Maréchaux. I'm going to print the photos. I have to call Marco later. I have a lot of things to do. Sometimes life rides along all by itself, there are several million of us like this, I'm riding, Marie's coming out tomorrow, I could ride for hours. I'm waiting for tomorrow. Well, there it is.

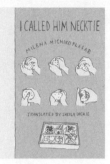

I Called Him Necktie by Milena Michiko Flašar

Twenty-year-old Taguchi Hiro has spent the last two years of his life living as a hikikomori—a shut-in who never leaves his room and has no human interaction—in his parents' home in Tokyo. As Hiro tentatively decides to reenter the world, he spends his days observing life from a park bench. Gradually he makes friends with Ohara Tetsu, a salaryman who has lost his job. The two discover in their sadness a common bond. This beautiful novel is moving, unforgettable, and full of surprises.

Who is Martha? by Marjana Gaponenko

In this rollicking novel, 96-year-old ornithologist Luka Levadski foregoes treatment for lung cancer and moves from Ukraine to Vienna to make a grand exit in a luxury suite at the Hotel Imperial. He reflects on his past while indulging in Viennese cakes and savoring music in a gilded concert hall. Levadski was born in 1914, the same year that Martha—the last of the now-extinct passenger pigeons—died. Levadski himself has an acute sense of being the last of a species. This gloriously written tale mixes piquant wit with lofty musings about life, friendship, aging and death.

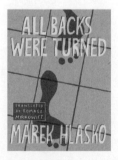

All Backs Were Turned by Marek Hlasko

Two desperate friends—on the edge of the law—travel to the southern Israeli city of Eilat to find work. There, Dov Ben Dov, the handsome native Israeli with a reputation for causing trouble, and Israel, his sidekick, stay with Ben Dov's younger brother, Little Dov, who has enough trouble of his own. Local toughs are encroaching on Little Dov's business, and he enlists his older brother to drive them away. It doesn't help that a beautiful German widow is rooming next door. A story of passion, deception, violence, and betrayal, conveyed in hardboiled prose reminiscent of Hammett and Chandler.

KILLING AUNTIE BY **ANDRZEJ BURSA**

A university student named Jurek finds himself with nothing to do. After his doting aunt asks the young man to perform a small chore, he decides to kill her for no good reason. This short comedic masterpiece combines elements of Dostoevsky, Sartre, Kafka and Heller to produce an unforgettable tale of murder and—just maybe—redemption.

ALEXANDRIAN SUMMER BY **YITZHAK GORMEZANO GOREN**

This is the story of two Jewish families living their frenzied last days in the doomed cosmopolitan social whirl of Alexandria just before fleeing Egypt for Israel in 1951. The conventions of the Egyptian upper-middle class are laid bare in this dazzling novel, which exposes sexual hypocrisies and portrays a vanished polyglot world of horse-racing, seaside promenades and nightclubs.

COCAINE BY **PITIGRILLI**

Paris in the 1920s – dizzy and decadent. Where a young man can make a fortune with his wits … unless he is led into temptation. Cocaine's dandified hero Tito Arnaudi invents lurid scandals and gruesome deaths, and sells these stories to the newspapers. But his own life becomes even more outrageous when he acquires three demanding mistresses. Elegant, witty and wicked, Pitigrilli's classic novel was first published in Italian in 1921 and retains its venom even today.

Some Day by Shemi Zarhin

On the shores of Israel's Sea of Galilee lies the city of Tiberias, a place bursting with sexuality and longing for love. The air is saturated with smells of cooking and passion. Some Day is a gripping family saga, a sensual and emotional feast that plays out over decades. This is an enchanting tale about tragic fates that disrupt families and break our hearts. Zarhin's hypnotic writing renders a painfully delicious vision of individual lives behind Israel's larger national story.

The Missing Year of Juan Salvatierra by Pedro Mairal

At the age of nine, Juan Salvatierra became mute following a horse riding accident. At twenty, he began secretly painting a series of canvases on which he detailed six decades of life in his village on Argentina's frontier with Uruguay. After his death, his sons return to deal with their inheritance: a shed packed with rolls over two miles long. But an essential roll is missing. A search ensues that illuminates links between art and life, with past family secrets casting their shadows on the present.

The Good Life Elsewhere by Vladimir Lorchenkov

The very funny - and very sad - story of a group of villagers and their tragicomic efforts to emigrate from Europe's most impoverished nation to Italy for work. An Orthodox priest is deserted by his wife for an art-dealing atheist; a mechanic redesigns his tractor for travel by air and sea; and thousands of villagers take to the road on a modern-day religious crusade to make it to the Italian Promised Land. A country where 25 percent of its population works abroad, remittances make up nearly 40 percent of GDP, and alcohol consumption per capita is the world's highest – Moldova surely has its problems. But, as Lorchenkov vividly shows, it's also a country whose residents don't give up easily.

KILLING THE SECOND DOG BY MAREK HLASKO

Two down-and-out Polish con men living in Israel in the 1950s scam an American widow visiting the country. Robert, who masterminds the scheme, and Jacob, who acts it out, are tough, desperate men, exiled from their native land and adrift in the hot, nasty underworld of Tel Aviv. Robert arranges for Jacob to run into the widow who has enough trouble with her young son to keep her occupied all day. What follows is a story of romance, deception, cruelty and shame. Hlasko's writing combines brutal realism with smoky, hardboiled dialogue, in a bleak world where violence is the norm and love is often only an act.

FANNY VON ARNSTEIN: DAUGHTER OF THE ENLIGHTENMENT BY HILDE SPIEL

In 1776 Fanny von Arnstein, the daughter of the Jewish master of the royal mint in Berlin, came to Vienna as an 18-year-old bride. She married a financier to the Austro-Hungarian imperial court, and hosted an ever more splendid salon which attracted luminaries of the day. Spiel's elegantly written and carefully researched biography provides a vivid portrait of a passionate woman who advocated for the rights of Jews, and illuminates a central era in European cultural and social history.

 New Vessel Press

To purchase these titles and for more information please visit
newvesselpress.com.